Praise for Buried Thunder

'A symphony of unease . . . this book won't make
you feel safe.'
Nicolette Jones, *Sunday Times*

'Carnegie-winner Bowler is on great form with this intense,
psychological thriller.'
The Bookseller

'A tense and haunting thriller.'
Julia Eccleshare, *Lovereading*

'An ingenious, fast-moving, highly readable gothic mystery.'
The School Librarian

'Frightening and well-paced . . . reminded me of
Alan Garner's classic *The Owl Service*.'
Geraldine Brennan, *The Observer*

'A powerfully atmospheric psychological thriller.'
Robert Dunbar, *Irish Times*

'Truly chilling.'
Bookbag

'*Buried Thunder* is a tour de force . . . teen fiction at its
very best.'
Lancashire Evening Post

BURIED
THUNDER

OTHER BOOKS BY TIM BOWLER

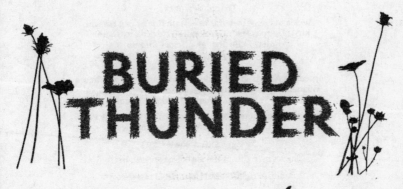

BURIED THUNDER

Tim Bowler

OXFORD
UNIVERSITY PRESS

OXFORD

UNIVERSITY PRESS

Great Clarendon Street, Oxford OX2 6DP
Oxford University Press is a department of the University of Oxford.
It furthers the University's objective of excellence in research, scholarship,
and education by publishing worldwide in

Oxford New York

Auckland Cape Town Dar es Salaam Hong Kong Karachi
Kuala Lumpur Madrid Melbourne Mexico City Nairobi
New Delhi Shanghai Taipei Toronto

With offices in

Argentina Austria Brazil Chile Czech Republic France Greece
Guatemala Hungary Italy Japan Poland Portugal Singapore
South Korea Switzerland Thailand Turkey Ukraine Vietnam

Oxford is a registered trade mark of Oxford University Press
in the UK and in certain other countries

British Library Cataloguing in Publication Data

Data available

ISBN: 978-0-19-272869-2

1 3 5 7 9 10 8 6 4 2

Printed in Great Britain

Paper used in the production of this book is a natural,
recyclable product made from wood grown in sustainable forests.
The manufacturing process conforms to the environmental
regulations of the country of origin.

For my mother and father
with love

'All things truly wicked start from an innocence'
Ernest Hemingway

1

The body was lying in a thicket—a woman of about thirty—and Maya wouldn't have noticed it at all if she hadn't tripped over a root and rolled up against it. She scrambled back to her feet and stared down. The figure lay motionless, dusk settling over it. From a distant part of the forest came the sound of Tom calling.

'Maya!'

'Tom!' she called back.

But she knew he couldn't hear her. She'd shouted repeatedly but his voice had continued to move further from her. He was clearly heading back to the village. He tried once more, even so.

'Where are you?'

That was the trouble. She didn't know. She didn't even remember how she'd ended up here. Something must have made her run away from Tom and cut into the trees, yet her mind was a shadow. She had a ghost of recollection.

Something on the path, something yellow.

But that was all.

She didn't shout back this time. She knew there was no point; and besides, she now had a bigger problem. She looked down at the body. She had to check this out, however scared she felt. There was just a chance this woman was alive. She took a slow breath, then knelt down.

The ground felt hard and bony. She peered at the body,

1

wary in case it suddenly moved, but all was still. She inched nearer, the dusk thickening around her. Even this close it was hard to make out the figure clearly, but gradually the image defined itself.

A curvy form, chest and stomach still, so too the face. Eyes shut. A blue dress, the colour just discernible in the fading light, and a low neckline. The woman seemed to have come from a party. There was no sign of an injury.

Something glinted in the darkness, a pendant nestling in the woman's cleavage: a horseshoe emblem on a slender chain. A lock of hair fell over it and then was still. Maya clenched her fists. This woman was surely dead.

And yet . . .

'Are you alive?' she said.

Her voice sounded small in the darkening forest. There was no response, but from somewhere near came a rustling sound. She whirled round and peered into the gloom. The rustling stopped and silence fell once more.

She could feel herself starting to panic. She thought of her mobile back at home. Not that it would help much here. She had no idea how to describe where she was. She'd barely found her way round Hembury village in the few days since the family moved here. The forest she didn't know at all.

The rustling came again.

Then faded as before.

She stood up. She had to find the path home, raise the alarm, and somehow memorize the way to this place, so that she could describe it to the police. She looked about her and straightaway found the perfect marker: a huge beech tree, clearly damaged. Even in this poor light she could see that two of the lower branches had been cut off and a third was supported by a cradle of ropes from above.

She looked back at the body on the ground.

'I'm going to run back home,' she whispered. She had no idea why she was talking to this woman. 'I'm going to find Mum and Dad, and they'll call the police. I'll run as fast as I can. You won't be on your own for long.'

It was then that she heard footsteps.

Not heavy. Quite the opposite. They sounded stealthy. She crouched, her eyes moving fast. This didn't have to be dangerous. It might even be someone who could help, someone who might miss all this and walk straight past if she didn't call out or show herself.

But she stayed where she was and said nothing.

The footsteps drew closer. She edged behind an oak tree and waited. Closer, closer, slow footsteps—then suddenly they stopped and silence fell once more. She stayed behind the oak, her ears straining.

But all she heard was a rustle in the leaves above her that died as she craned her head round to look. The foliage was still, as though it had never moved. She turned and gazed back at the dead woman.

Still lying in the same position, but something looked different. Then she saw it. The head had tilted to the side, the long hair falling away, and the eyes were now open; and underneath them—like a third eye—the horseshoe pendant was shining in the darkness.

Maya stared. She wanted to run so much, but she found she couldn't move. The pendant went on shining, and something in the dead eyes seemed to shine too. She swallowed. This was madness. She had to break free.

She slipped from behind the oak and crept towards the edge of the thicket. The dusk was now so heavy it was hard to see anything clearly, but somehow she made out the way to go. She stole forward, watching, listening.

Here was the clearing. She remembered stumbling into it on her mad rush here. To the left was the damaged beech tree; to the right the deeper, denser folds of the forest. It was hard to believe she'd crashed through that, yet remembered so little of it.

But that was the way she had to go. She knew that much at least. The path home lay somewhere in that direction. She took a deep breath and set off across the clearing—only to freeze once again.

A second body was lying before her.

Straight ahead.

She made herself creep closer. She had to check this out too. She knew it. She couldn't just run past, however much she wanted to. It was a man this time, and like the woman, clearly dead. She knelt beside him. No movement in the stomach or chest. The eyes were open but they were vacant.

Once again, there was no sign of an injury.

She was trembling now. She forced herself to study the body. The police would ask questions. They'd want a description. She tried to take in what she could, muttering what she saw into the silent air.

'Man about thirty-five, suit, tie, white shirt, red hair . . .'

She stopped, looked again. But there was no mistake. The darkness was draining all colour from the body, yet something red still clung to the hair.

'Red hair,' she went on, 'and . . . and a silver watch.'

Something was moving over to the right, a shadow among the trees at the top of the clearing. She narrowed her eyes and stared; but the shadow was gone and all was gloom again. She tried to stay calm, make herself think.

There were probably lots of paths back to the village but she didn't know them. She had to find the way she'd come, and that meant heading for the trees, whatever else lay in that direction; and she had to go now. She set off across the clearing, walking fast.

She wanted to run. She wanted to burst through the trees and away from this place, but she knew she had to resist. All her instincts told her that the moment she broke into a run, panic would take over. A fast, steady walk was what was needed. Yet even as she walked, she felt a pressure to look back.

She ignored it. She had to scan the trees, watch for danger, find the path, get away. She mustn't look back. Just keep walking, walking, walking. She strode on, step, step, step, but still the pressure grew. She stopped, breathing hard, and turned.

The man's body was still visible, lying on its back, but as with the woman, the head had tilted to the side and the eyes were shining in the darkness. She turned and hurried on towards the trees—only to freeze yet again.

The shadow was back, directly in front of her. The features were hidden, the form blurred, but there was no mistaking the figure standing there, back towards her, bent over a third body stretched upon the forest floor.

She stared, and as she did so, she saw the figure stiffen, as though it had sensed her, and straighten, and turn towards her. But she saw no more. She was running wild, blundering through thickets, coppices, tawny shrubs.

She had no idea where she was going. All she knew was that she was crashing through branches, brambles, foliage. She heard shouts. Some were hers, some were not. She couldn't catch the words.

They came again, somewhere near. She thought of the shadow and raced on. The shouts continued but she was hardly listening now. All she wanted was to run, run, run. But she didn't know which way to go. Then she saw it. Straight ahead.

She stopped, gasping, and peered into the darkness. Before her was a wall of trees—and something else. Two

5

yellow eyes, watching her; and now a head, and a body. Then she saw what it was.

A fox.

Recollection came streaming back. She'd seen a fox earlier, perhaps this very one. She remembered it now. It had been on the path and she'd followed it into the forest, leaving Tom behind. But why had she done that? And why had she forgotten about it till now?

'What do you want?' she heard herself say.

The yellow eyes closed, opened, closed again.

And in the space where they had been, she saw a narrow path through the trees.

She tore down it, screaming. But here were the shouts again, and they were closer than ever. She ran on, on, the voices growing louder—and then she fell. She saw leaves, branches, the trunk of a tree, the face of the forest floor as she tumbled upon it.

And a shadow leaning over her.

2

'Maya,' it said.

A light flashed out. She twisted round and peered up into the beam of a torch.

'Dad?' she said.

'Maya, what's happened?'

But before she could answer, he turned and bellowed into the darkness.

'She's over here!'

An answering call came. Mum's voice—and it was close.

'Maya!'

A moment later Mum was there, also with a torch.

'Sweetheart!' Mum knelt down. 'Are you hurt?'

'No, I'm—'

'Come here.'

Maya pushed herself up into Mum's arms. Mum held her close, whispering.

'It's all right. It's all right.'

Dad shouted into the darkness again.

'Tom! We're over here!'

Maya pushed her face into the folds of Mum's jacket, crying softly now. She heard more shouts, Dad calling directions to Tom and answers flying back. A few moments later a third torch brushed over her.

'Sis!' said Tom. 'You all right?'

She didn't answer.

'What can I do?' he said. 'Tell me what I can do.'

'Turn the torch off, can you? It's blinding me.'

Mum, Dad, and Tom turned their torches off. Maya shuddered. She hadn't meant them all to do it, just Tom. But she said nothing and let the darkness close around them.

'We ought to be getting back,' said Dad.

'Maya's not ready yet,' said Mum. 'Give her a bit longer.'

'OK.'

The darkness deepened. Maya thought of the fox she'd seen just a short while ago: the same animal—surely—as the one that had led her to the bodies; the fox she'd then inexplicably forgotten. She wouldn't forget it again.

Mum kissed her.

'Do you want to tell us what happened? Or would you rather get home and talk there?'

Maya didn't need to think. The story rushed out of her. She told them about the dead woman, the dead man, the third body, the figure standing over it. Dad pulled out his mobile and was soon talking to the police.

'My daughter, yes . . . Maya Munro . . . she's fourteen . . .'

Maya dipped her head into Mum's shoulder again. Dad went through the story, leaving nothing out.

'I can ask her,' he said suddenly.

Maya looked up at him but he was still talking into the phone.

'Only she probably won't be able to give you much more than what I've just told you. We only moved to Hembury a few days ago. We've taken over the old hotel just up from the village square. Yes . . . The Rowan Tree. But the point is, we don't know our way round yet, especially the forest. So Maya's hardly going to be able to tell you where she was. OK, OK. I'll ask her.'

Dad put a hand over the phone.

'Maya,' he whispered, 'they want to know exactly

where the bodies are. No pressure if you can't give me anything, but are there any details you can remember?'

She told him about the thicket, the clearing, the damaged beech tree.

'That might help,' he said.

He touched her cheek.

'Well done.'

He took a few steps from them and continued the call.

Tom knelt down. 'Sis?'

She knew what was coming.

'Why did you run away from me?'

'I don't know. I—'

'It's not like you.'

'I'm sorry.'

'You just ran off down the path,' said Tom. 'You disappeared round the bend and when I got there and looked for you, you'd vanished. I kept calling for you but you didn't answer. I never thought you'd shoot off into the forest so I ran back to The Rowan Tree.'

She wondered how she could explain herself, not just to Tom but to Mum and Dad. She'd told them about the bodies, but she'd said nothing about the fox. She wasn't sure why.

'Time for talking later,' said Mum.

Maya looked round but Mum's eyes were not on her. They were searching the darkness, and Tom's were now doing the same. Dad was still talking on the phone but he too was checking shadows. She thought of the figure she'd seen bent over the third body: the figure that had sensed her and turned.

'OK,' said Dad. 'Thanks very much.'

He put the mobile away, flicked on his torch and walked back to join them.

'Come on.' He pulled Maya gently to her feet. 'Home.'

'What about the police?' she said.

'They'll check out the bodies.'

'But don't they need to ask questions?'

'Yes.' Dad put an arm round her. 'But not now and not here. Come on.'

They set off through the forest, all torches on again. She looked about her, trying to recognize something from before. But it was no good. If she'd come this way earlier, she must have been running too scared to notice anything.

Then she saw the stile.

Here at last was something she remembered. She'd climbed over this when she'd entered the forest. So she had come this way. She stared over at the path beyond. That too was familiar. She'd walked along it with Tom, then, for a reason that made no sense, she'd left it behind.

And him.

She thought of the fox again.

'Come on,' said Dad. 'Let's not hang around.'

She climbed over the stile onto the path. The others followed and they set off in the direction of Hembury village. The silence felt as heavy as the darkness. The path wound on, forest on either side, then the trees to the right fell away and fields opened up.

She felt only partial relief. It was good to see the church and the stone cottages that hugged the outskirts of the village, but the forest to the left looked darker and denser than ever. She thought of the bodies and hurried on.

There were three police cars and an ambulance in the square, and a knot of villagers gathered round.

'Keep walking,' said Dad.

'What about the police?' said Mum. 'Shouldn't we make ourselves known to them?'

Dad shook his head.

'I told the officer we'll talk back at home. And that's what we're going to do. I don't want people pestering Maya out here.'

He led them round the back of The Rose and Crown and up the lane towards The Rowan Tree. Maya stared at the ancient building. The lights were on in most of the windows and the rising moon was already brightening the thatch; yet the hotel seemed strangely sombre.

She saw Tom watching her.

'You're still angry with me,' she said.

'You're not yourself, sis.'

'Tom,' said Dad, 'not now.'

Tom took no notice.

'You're not yourself. And I'll tell you something else— you were weird back on the path. When we went out walking.'

'What do you mean?'

'There was something you said. Just before you ran off.'

'What was it?'

'Can't you remember?'

She tried to picture the path just before she'd run off. She could see it in her mind, but the next thing she remembered was finding the woman's body. What had happened in-between was a blur.

Apart from the yellow eyes.

'We were searching for owls,' said Tom.

She bit her lip. Of course. It was owls.

'It was getting dusky,' said Tom. 'Remember?'

'Yes.'

'Do you really remember or are you just saying yes?'

'I really remember.'

'Then tell me what happened,' he said. 'Tell me what we were doing. And don't just say we were searching for owls, because I've already told you that.'

11

'Tom,' said Mum. 'Ease up a bit.'

Tom said nothing. Maya hesitated.

'We set off from The Rowan Tree,' she said. 'I remember that. You said it was a good time to see owls hunting. We . . . we walked down to where the fields end and . . . we carried on down the path with the trees on either side. Where we've just come back from. And we walked on for a while, looking for owls. Only we didn't see any so . . .'

She paused, picturing the memories.

'So we turned back and headed for home again. You said we mustn't get caught out after dark because we don't know our way round yet. And . . . I guess that's when I ran on ahead and left you behind.'

Tom gave a snort.

'Yeah, right.'

'Tom,' said Dad. 'That's enough now. Come on, Maya.'

He started to lead her up to the entrance of The Rowan Tree. But Tom caught her arm and stopped her.

'You left something out,' he said.

'Tom,' said Dad. 'Let go of Maya's arm.'

Tom let go. But he stepped in front of her.

'You left something out.'

'If I did,' she said, 'it's because I've forgotten it.'

Tom gave her a baleful look.

'We did see an owl,' he said. 'It was perched on one of the fence posts along the side of the path. Just up from that stile.'

She tried to picture it. She could see the path, the stile, the fence posts, the trees beyond: the trees into which she'd run. But no owl.

'Maybe it was just you who saw the owl,' she said.

'You saw it too. You pointed it out to me.'

She felt Mum and Dad stiffen nearby.

12

'You pointed it out,' said Tom. 'We started to walk down towards it, just a few steps to get a better look. But then you wanted to stop. Not too close, you said, or we'll disturb it. Remember? We had a bit of an argument. I wanted to go closer and you said stay or we'll frighten it off.'

She shook her head, unable to see it. Then suddenly the picture floated into her mind.

'I remember,' she said. 'I didn't want us to go closer, but I was lying about not wanting to frighten the owl. The owl wasn't frightened at all. I didn't want to go closer because I was the one who was frightened.'

She searched her mind again.

'I caught you by the arm,' she said. 'Like you caught mine just now.'

'And then?'

'The owl flew off.'

'That's right.'

'Tom,' said Mum. 'Enough now.'

Tom shook his head.

'There's more.'

'Enough now.'

'Mum,' he said, 'there's something important. Maya, tell them.'

Maya stared at him.

'But . . . I can't remember . . .'

'The owl flew off,' he said. 'You just said you remember that.'

'Yes.'

'Which way did it go?'

'I . . . I . . .'

'Which way did it go?'

'Into the trees.'

'Which direction?'

'The way the . . . ' She shivered. 'The way the bodies were.'

'And then what happened?'

'I can't remember.'

'Think!'

'Tom,' said Dad. 'Leave it.'

'She's OK.' Tom looked hard at her. 'Sis, tell Dad you're OK.'

She didn't answer. She was searching her mind again. The image of the owl was clear now. She could see it ghosting into the trees, swallowed by grey. Then nothing.

'I can't remember, Tom.'

'You said something.'

'What?'

'You said something. Just after the owl flew off. Do you remember what that was?'

She shook her head. Tom's eyes flickered over her.

'You said, "Someone's going to die".'

He paused.

'Do you remember that?'

'No.'

'It freaked me out. And you said it in this strange voice. Kind of a faraway voice. I told myself you must be talking about the owl hunting for its dinner. But you didn't mean that, did you? You said someone, not something. You meant a person. Or more than one person.'

Tom glanced at Mum and Dad, then back at Maya.

'Three maybe.'

She looked down.

'I'm sorry,' she said.

'There's nothing to be sorry for,' said Mum.

'I just . . . don't remember saying that.'

'It doesn't matter,' said Dad.

Yet again she pictured the path. She saw the owl

14

flying off. It was sharp in her memory now and surely, she thought, if she was patient, the words would come back too. But no words came. All that came was another image—of yellow eyes drawing her into the trees: the way the owl had flown.

'Let's go in,' said Dad.

He stepped up to the front door.

'The police are here already,' he said, peering through the glass. 'One of them anyway. I can see a uniform.'

He opened the door and walked in. Maya stood back and let Mum and Tom go ahead of her, and for a moment she lingered outside, aware of a new fear that she couldn't account for. The others blocked her view of the reception area, but then they stepped aside and she saw through the open door a policewoman studying one of the paintings on the far wall.

'Can I help you?' said Dad.

The woman turned with a smile, and Maya shivered again.

It was the woman she'd seen lying dead in the forest.

3

There was no mistake. Unless it was a twin, this was the woman she'd seen earlier, though not in the blue dress, nor was her hair falling free; and if she was wearing the horseshoe pendant, it was hidden by the uniform.

'Good evening,' she said to Dad. 'I'm WPC Shaw.'

'Phil Munro. This is my wife Paula.'

The two women nodded.

'My son Tom,' Dad went on.

'Hello, Tom,' said the policewoman. 'And how old are you?'

Tom grunted.

'Fifteen.'

'And this is Maya,' said Dad.

'Hello, Maya.'

Maya said nothing. She could only stare. WPC Shaw's eyes flicked over her, then settled on Dad again.

'I understand you've taken over The Rowan Tree,' she said.

'That's right. We just moved in a few days ago.'

'Nice to see the hotel open again after being empty for so many months. And you seem to have quite a few guests already.'

'We're filling up,' said Dad. 'Haven't got any staff yet so we're having to do everything ourselves for the moment. But we're getting there. Listen . . . '

He slipped an arm round Maya.

16

'I know you've got lots of questions for Maya, but can you just give her a bit of time first? She's had a horrible experience and she's very shaken up. I want to get some food inside her. And a hot drink.'

'Of course,' said the policewoman. 'I'm not here to ask questions anyway. My colleagues are checking out the forest and I was just sent to ask you all to stay on the premises till they get here.'

'OK,' said Dad. 'We'll be in the kitchen.'

'I'll wait here.'

'Sit in the lounge if you want.'

'Here's fine.'

'Cup of tea?'

'Don't worry. You take care of Maya.'

But Maya was already hurrying towards the kitchen. Anything to get away from WPC Shaw. She also yearned for solitude. She needed to think, not just about this woman but the other forms she'd seen in the forest: the red-haired man, the third body, the figure standing over it. Perhaps WPC Shaw's colleagues would turn out to be these people.

Anything seemed possible right now.

But the police officers who turned up were nothing like the figures she'd seen. Two men and a woman, and even allowing for the poor visibility in the forest, she knew these three were different. They sat down at the far end of the kitchen table and Mum put mugs of tea in front of them.

'Thank you, Mrs Munro,' said the woman.

Mum sat down between Tom and Dad. Maya pushed her untouched food away and waited, glad that WPC Shaw hadn't come through but wary of the three officers in front of her.

'I'm DI Henderson,' said the older of the two men. 'This

17

gentleman is DC Coker. And this is WPC Becket.'

'Thank you for coming out so quickly,' said Mum.

'No problem at all.' DI Henderson turned to DC Coker. 'Annie doesn't need to hang around. Tell her she can go.'

DC Coker left the room, and a moment later Maya caught the sound of voices and the click of the front door. On an impulse she glanced towards the window, and there was WPC Shaw walking down the lane towards the village square.

She stared after her.

Annie Shaw.

So that was the name of the woman who was meant to be dead.

DC Coker rejoined them.

'Now then,' said DI Henderson. 'I think we need to hear the story from Maya's own lips.'

Maya looked round at him, her mind still on Annie Shaw, and on what she knew they'd all think if she told them the truth. If indeed she knew the truth. She was no longer certain about anything.

'Take your time, Maya,' said the policeman.

She took a slow breath.

'What did you find in the forest?' she said.

'We'll tell you in a moment,' said the officer. 'When you've filled us in on your side of things.'

'But Dad's already told you what I saw.'

'We'd like to hear your version of events.'

'Am I in trouble?'

'No, no,' said DI Henderson. 'Nothing like that. We just want to hear the story from your own lips.'

She looked into the policeman's eyes, aware that they hadn't left her face for a second. She could feel the others watching too. The officer smiled; but it didn't feel reassuring. It felt like a trap.

'Just tell us what happened, Maya.'

She started to speak. She told them about the path, the owl, the words she'd muttered to Tom; the stumble into the forest, the first body, the second, the third, the figure standing over it; the dash through the trees; Dad finding her. She told them everything she could remember.

Except the part about the fox.

And the identity of the dead woman.

She knew she couldn't do either. She wasn't sure why.

But it made no difference anyway. Even as she talked, she could see no one believed her. DC Coker was making notes but when he looked up at the end and smiled, she could tell he thought she was wasting everyone's time.

'All done, Maya?' he said.

'Yes.'

'Nothing to add?'

'No.'

She caught Tom's eye, but he looked away. Dad leaned on the table and stared at the three officers.

'Did you have any problems finding the place Maya described?'

'None at all,' said DI Henderson. 'Moment you mentioned the damaged beech tree we knew where she meant.'

'So what did you see there?'

'Nobody.'

The policeman turned to Maya.

'Or rather, no bodies,' he went on, emphasizing each word. 'Since that's what you say you saw.' He paused. 'And is that what you saw?'

Maya looked down.

'I'm not accusing you of anything,' said the officer. 'It was getting dark so things must have been hard to see. Easy to make a mistake and—'

'I saw the bodies.' She looked up at him. 'I did.'

DI Henderson watched her impassively. She glanced at the other two officers. WPC Becket was picking hairs from her cuff; DC Coker was yawning. She saw Mum and Dad forcing unnatural smiles at her. Tom spoke suddenly.

'Maya's telling the truth.'

No one answered.

'She is,' he said. 'She never tells lies. She's the most truthful person you'll ever meet.'

The policewoman looked up for a moment, then returned to the hairs on her cuff.

'Maya,' said DI Henderson, 'we're not accusing you of lying.'

'Yes, you are,' said Tom. 'You're making her sound like—'

'Tom,' said Mum. 'Let the gentleman speak.'

'But—'

'Let him speak.'

DI Henderson glanced at Tom.

'I'm not gunning for your sister.'

'You are,' said Tom. 'You're making her sound like she's a basket-case.'

'I'm just trying to clear up what appears to be a contradiction,' said the officer. 'Maya reports three bodies—'

'And a figure.'

'And a figure. But so far we haven't been able to substantiate any of those things.'

'What does "substantiate" mean?' said Tom.

'It means we haven't found any proof of what she saw.'

Again Maya pictured Annie Shaw: the Annie Shaw who'd smiled, the Annie Shaw whose dead eyes had followed her through the forest; and she thought of those other eyes—the yellow ones—and wondered where they were now.

For some reason they felt close.

'So, Maya,' said DI Henderson.

The policeman was watching her again.

'You say you knelt by the woman and the red-haired man.'

'Yes.'

'And you were sure they were dead.'

'Yes.'

'Have you had any medical training? First aid lessons at school? Something like that?'

Maya bit her lip.

'No.'

'Have you ever examined a dead body before?'

'No.'

'Did you check for a pulse?'

Maya hesitated.

'Maya?' said the officer.

'Nothing was moving,' she said. 'The chest and the stomach, they were—'

'Did you check for a pulse, Maya?'

She stared back at the policeman.

'No,' she said quietly.

DI Henderson drummed his fingers on the table.

'But they were dead,' she said. 'The woman and the red-haired man.'

'Maybe.'

'Not maybe,' said Tom. 'Definitely. If Maya says they were dead—'

'Yes, yes.' DI Henderson glanced at him. 'We've established that your sister never tells lies. And I repeat what I just said. Maybe.'

Maya felt Mum take her hand. DI Henderson's eye softened slightly.

'All I'm trying to do, Maya, is find an explanation that

21

fits both stories. What you saw and what we saw, OK?'

'OK.'

'So for example, I'm asking myself, what if these people were drunk? You say they were dressed up, like they'd been to a party. Well, maybe they'd had too much to drink, went staggering off into the forest, got separated. The woman collapses first, the red-haired man blunders about, trying to find her, then he collapses too.'

'What about the third body?' said Mum. 'And the figure standing over it?'

'Same as the first two,' said DI Henderson. 'They all get drunk at the party and stagger out into the forest. The woman collapses first, then the red-haired man, then the third member of the group. Fourth member leans over to check if Number Three's OK. Maya sees all this, panics and runs off. By the time we get there, they've all come round and walked off. It does fit.'

'No, it doesn't,' said Maya.

'Why not?'

'Because the woman . . . '

She stopped, staring ahead; and from somewhere in her mind the face of Annie Shaw seemed to stare back: first as an officer, then as a corpse.

'What about the woman?' said DI Henderson.

'She was exactly like . . . '

'Like what?'

Maya closed her eyes; but the image of Annie Shaw remained.

'Like a dead person,' she said.

4

Night-time and the solitude she craved. The last of the guests had turned in; voices were stilled, televisions switched off. The Rowan Tree was silent; but her mind was screaming.

She sat down on the bed and tried to relax, but it was no use. She was on her feet again almost at once. She glanced at the clock: one in the morning. She'd been in her room since eleven and she was still dressed, still pacing the floor.

'Get into bed,' she told herself. 'At least do that.'

She pulled off her clothes, dumped them on the chair, stared at her reflection in the mirror. Her face seemed pale, pinched, almost alien. A shiver ran over her. She looked round, wary of everything now, including this new home.

She still wasn't sure what it was about The Rowan Tree that she didn't like. She felt she ought to love it. Mum and Dad did; so did Tom, and she could understand why: a romantic country hotel, dating from the fourteenth century. The place had everything going for it. But she'd felt uneasy here from the start.

Though she'd said nothing.

She slipped on her nightie, walked over to the window and peered through a gap in the curtains. All was black at first but gradually it eased and she made out the lane stretching away towards the village square, the houses on either side, their low walls, front gardens, even the hanging baskets; and further down, the shrouded shapes of The Rose and Crown, the primary school, and old Hembury church.

The forest was too dark to see.

Something rapped at the door of her room. She stared towards it, listening hard. The rap came again. She took a deep breath, walked up to the door, and pulled it open.

'Maya,' said a voice.

She slumped against the side of the door.

It was Tom, standing there in his pyjamas.

'You OK, sis?'

She pulled him into the room and closed the door behind them.

'Why aren't you sleeping?' she said.

'Why aren't you?'

She didn't answer.

'I'm sorry I bit your head off earlier,' said Tom.

She shrugged.

'I'm sorry I ran away. I didn't mean to scare you.'

'You scared yourself more,' said Tom. 'But I was scared for you. I still am.'

'I'm OK.'

'No, you're not. You've been pacing up and down.'

'How do you know?'

'I heard you. I can't sleep either. I've been wandering about The Rowan Tree, thinking of all the stuff you told the police. And I heard you walking up and down, so I came to see if you're all right.'

'Thanks.' She looked away. 'Tommy?'

'Yeah?'

'I know you don't believe me about the bodies. And I don't blame you. Or Mum and Dad. They don't believe me either.'

24

'They never said that.'

'They don't anyway. But it's OK. I understand. It must sound crazy, what I said. Specially when the police didn't find anything.'

'Sis?'

She looked back at him.

'It doesn't matter,' he said, 'about us believing you or not. What matters is we stick together, OK?'

'Yeah, I know.'

She pulled him close and they held each other for a few moments, then he pulled back.

'There's something I meant to tell you,' he said.

'What?'

'About that policewoman. WPC Shaw.'

Maya stiffened.

'What about her?'

'I don't trust her,' said Tom. 'You remember when we got back, she was waiting for us in the reception area?'

'Yeah.'

'And she was all chatty and stuff? And Dad said we were going to get some food inside you and she could go through to the lounge if she wanted to? And she said she was OK staying in the reception area? You remember all that?'

'Yeah, yeah.'

'Well, I'll tell you something.' Tom leaned closer. 'When we were all sitting in the kitchen, I caught sight of her through a gap in the door.'

'I thought the kitchen door was closed.'

'It wasn't. It was ajar. I don't know which one of us came through last—'

'Mum did.'

'Well, she didn't close it properly, and I could see through the gap all the way down the corridor to the reception

25

area. I only spotted the gap after we'd been sitting with you for a while. But I could see what that policewoman was doing. You know what it was?'

Tom didn't wait for an answer.

'She was searching the reception area. I saw her clearly. She was turning things over, checking behind vases, looking under cushions.'

'Did she see you watching her?'

'Don't think so.'

'How long was she doing that?'

'Don't know. Like I say, I only spotted the door was ajar after we'd been sitting in the kitchen for a while. She might have been poking about all the time we were in there and I never knew. Maybe even before we got back from the forest. She was waiting for us, remember?'

'Did you tell Mum and Dad about this?'

'No,' said Tom. 'Do you think I should have done?'

'Don't know.'

Tom yawned.

'There's probably nothing to it,' he said. 'Maybe it's just what police do. Check stuff over. They probably think they've got a right to. I can't believe the woman's a crook. But I don't trust her.'

He yawned again. Maya touched him on the arm.

'Go to bed, Tommy. I'm all right now.'

'You sure?'

'Yeah. Thanks for looking out for me. Like you always do.'

Tom said nothing. She hesitated.

'You didn't let me down,' she said. 'Back on the path.'

'I did.'

'No, you didn't. I let you down. By running away. It wasn't your fault, what happened. It was mine.'

She kissed him on the cheek.

'Night, sis,' he said.

She closed the door and listened to Tom's footsteps padding away. She still wasn't ready for bed. She knew there was no point. She was more worked up than ever.

Nothing made sense; nothing seemed real. Maybe the others were right not to believe her. Maybe she really had imagined everything, not just Annie Shaw's return from the dead, but the other figures in the forest.

She pulled on her dressing gown. There was one thing she could do. It was probably a waste of time and she was a little nervous about leaving her room, but she had to try this. She eased open the door again and stepped out.

The corridor was dark but she set off down it, feeling for things to hold. She still wasn't sure where all the light switches were at The Rowan Tree, but she knew there was one at the far end on the left.

Here it was. She reached out to flick it on, then changed her mind. No point in waking other people, and besides, she didn't want to draw attention to herself right now. She reached the top of the staircase and felt her way down to the ground floor.

The lower corridors were dark too. She crept through to the reception area and stopped by the desk. Nothing looked out of place. The pens and pencils were in the mug; the diary was exactly where Dad always left it.

She glanced round. All seemed normal, but she ought to do this properly; and this time she would put the light on. She flicked the switch. The sudden brightness made her feel vulnerable, but she mastered this and started to check round.

Annie Shaw had been searching for something.

What was it?

There seemed to be no clues at all. Everything was exactly as it had been. She walked over to the paintings

27

on the far wall. The policewoman had been staring at those when they'd arrived back at The Rowan Tree. But there was nothing she could see in the old watercolours that made things any clearer.

This was stupid. She could stand here all night and get nowhere. She switched off the light—and at once caught a glint in the darkness. Down on the floor, directly beneath the picture of Hembury church: something small and bright. She bent down.

There was no need to switch on the light again. The object was caught in the pile of the carpet and it was shining in the darkness. She leaned closer and suddenly saw what it was.

The horseshoe pendant.

She closed her hand round it and stood up. As she did so, she felt a jet of cold air from the direction of the front door. She glanced towards it and saw in the glass a flash of yellow from the lane; it lingered for a moment, and then was gone.

She hurried back to her room, closed the door behind her and sat down on the bed. She was breathing hard. She waited, willing herself to calm down; then she un-curled her fingers and stared at the pendant sitting in her palm.

'You exist,' she murmured.

She felt round it, tracing the curve.

'You're real.'

She pictured the figures in the forest.

'And they're real too. I did see them.'

She closed her hand round the pendant again.

'You're proof.'

She squeezed it tight. She had to keep this, even though it wasn't hers. But no one else must know. She looked quickly around her. Under the pillow, under the mattress, inside a drawer—none of these places seemed safe. Her pockets were risky too.

She thought for a moment, then reached down to the skirting board behind the head of the bed and prised at the edge of the carpet. To her relief it peeled back easily to reveal a knotty floorboard underneath. She felt round the side of it, praying it would be loose.

It was. She raised the board just enough to peer through the gap. Below was the perfect hiding place: dark and dry, a little secret cupboard. She dropped the pendant through, replaced the board and carpet, then lay back on the bed, breathing hard again; and then she heard it.

In the silence.

Scratch, scratch, scratch.

Somewhere near. She sat up, trembling.

But all was quiet again.

5

Morning brought no relief.

'Maya,' said Mum, bent over the cooker. 'Table Four.'

'Forget Table Four,' said Tom, bursting into the kitchen. 'Do Table Six. They've been waiting for ages and the guy's getting prickly.'

'OK,' said Maya.

'All right, sweetheart?' said Mum.

'No problem.'

She hurried into the dining room and over to Table Six. Four figures stared up at her. Dimly she recognized them: the family who'd arrived two days ago. But they looked like ghosts. If the man was prickly, she couldn't see it in his face.

But she heard it in his voice.

'I was starting to think you'd forgotten us,' he growled.

'I'm really sorry,' she said. 'We're a bit short-staffed at the moment.'

She gazed round the dining room. Most of the tables were occupied, yet the room felt strangely silent. She could hear the flow of talk, the clink and clatter of cutlery and china, yet the sounds seemed muted.

She remembered the silence of the night.

The scratching.

The silence again.

The man grunted.

'Well, we can sit here all day,' he muttered, 'but it might

be nice if you asked us what we'd like for breakfast.'

'I'm sorry,' she said quickly. 'I thought you were still checking the menu.'

'If you'd been looking at us rather than staring round the room, you'd know that's a pretty stupid thing to say,' said the man. 'Anyway, let's get on with it.'

She wrote down the order and hurried back to the kitchen. Mum glanced at the chit and shook her head.

'Oh, Maya,' she said. 'I'm so sorry.'

'What do you mean?'

'I should never have asked you to do this.'

Mum held up the order chit.

'Can you make sense of that? Because I can't.'

Maya stared at it. Her handwriting—usually so neat—was illegible.

'Mum, I . . . '

'It's OK,' said Mum. 'It's totally, totally OK.'

Tom appeared with a tray of cups and saucers.

'Tom,' said Mum. 'Sort Table Six, can you?'

'Maya just took their order.'

'Can you do it again?'

Tom dumped the tray and looked at Maya.

'You all right, sis?'

'Maya's taking a break,' said Mum.

'But it's crazy in there,' said Tom. 'We need everyone we can get.'

'Maya's taking a break.'

'So what's Dad doing?'

'He's on the phone.'

'Can't that wait?' said Tom.

'No, it can't.'

'Is it about the loan?'

'Never mind what it's about,' said Mum. 'Sort Table Six, can you?'

Tom disappeared into the dining room. Maya let Mum steer her into the hall.

'I'm sorry, Mum,' she said.

'Nothing to be sorry about.'

'I'm letting everyone down.'

'No, you're not.'

Mum took her hands and squeezed them.

'It's my fault, not yours,' she said. 'I just thought, you know, after that nasty experience yesterday, it might take your mind off things to be busy. I should have been more sensitive. And I haven't even asked you how you slept last night.'

Before Maya could answer, there was a harsh ringing sound.

She jumped.

'Easy,' said Mum. 'It's only the door bell.'

'It sounds so loud.'

Mum kissed her.

'Take a break. Go on. We'll manage here. But check the front door on your way, can you? Your dad's tied up.'

'Is Tom right?' said Maya. 'Is it about the loan?'

'It might be.'

'Are we in trouble?'

'I don't know about trouble,' said Mum, 'but . . . '

'But what?'

Mum hesitated.

'Tell me,' said Maya.

'Well, put it this way,' said Mum, 'we borrowed a hell of a lot to get The Rowan Tree, and now we need the hotel to start making money. As quickly as possible. But that's not for you to worry about. Go and answer the door. And then take a break.'

Maya made her way down the hall. Dad was in the little office at the back of the reception area, hunched over the phone. He caught sight of her and gestured towards the front door. She opened it and saw a girl of about fifteen standing there, small and slim with black untidy hair offset by sharp blue eyes.

'I've come about the job,' she said.

Maya stared at her. 'What job?'

'In the kitchen.'

'I didn't know we'd advertised a job.'

'Are you saying you don't need any help?'

'I didn't say that. I mean . . . '

She looked round at Dad, still bent over the phone, his back now to her. She turned to the girl again.

'Where did you see the advert?'

The girl shrugged.

'I didn't. Just figured you'd be looking for help in the kitchen. I can go if you don't want me.'

Maya tried to think. She knew Mum and Dad planned to advertise for staff, yet this girl looked wild; and there was another problem. She didn't appear to be alone. Standing in the lane just a short way behind her was a large, ungainly boy, also about fifteen. His eyes were fixed on the girl, and he too looked wild.

'Don't worry about him,' said the girl. 'He's no trouble.'

'Who is he?'

'I'm Bonny,' came the answer.

Maya stared at the girl, unsure what to say. Bonny watched her for a few moments, then rolled her eyes.

'I'm going,' she said. 'You obviously don't need any help.'

'Wait,' said Maya.

The boy in the lane went on staring at the girl's back. Maya looked at him: a brute in terms of size and strength and he had the strangest eyes—not piercing like the girl's but dark and intense.

'Like I say,' said Bonny, 'I'm going.'

And she spun round and started to walk towards the boy.

'Wait!' called Maya. 'We do need someone in the kitchen. But you need to speak to my dad.'

The girl stopped and looked round. The boy had taken a step towards her; he now took a step back. Bonny took no notice of him and walked up to the door again.

'That your dad on the phone?' she said, peering in.

'Yes.'

'I'll wait till he's free.'

Maya hesitated, aware once again of the boy in the lane, now watching Bonny more fixedly than ever.

'I told you,' said the girl, 'he's no trouble.'

She called over her shoulder.

'Wait for me by the church!'

The boy stiffened.

'Wait for me by the church!' Bonny turned and faced him. 'Sit on the bench outside the gate. Wait till half past ten.'

The boy looked down at his watch.

'Wait till half past ten,' said Bonny. 'If I'm not there by half past ten, come back and stand here. Exactly where you are now. And I'll come out and tell you what to do next. Off you go.'

The boy was still staring at his watch.

'Half past ten,' said Bonny.

He looked up at her. She gave a nod in the direction of the square.

'Half past ten.'

The boy checked his watch yet again, then heaved himself round and lumbered off down the lane. Bonny watched him for a moment, then turned back to Maya.

'You're Maya,' she said.

'How do you know?'

'Not very difficult. You going to just stand there?'

Maya stood aside and Bonny stepped in. Dad put the phone down at the same moment and slipped out of the office. Bonny walked up to the reception desk.

'Morning,' she said.

'Morning.'

'I'm Bonny.'

'Phil Munro.'

'I know who you are.'

'You do?'

'Your wife's called Paula. You've got a son called Tom. And I've met Maya.'

'Done your homework,' said Dad.

'Small village,' said Bonny. 'Stuff gets around.'

'But we've only been here a few days.'

'So?'

Bonny's eyes flicked round the room for a moment, then fixed on Dad again.

'Do you want some help in the kitchen?' she said.

'You're very blunt.'

'Is that a problem?'

'Not necessarily.' Dad leaned on the desk. 'What kind of help were you thinking of?'

'Whatever.'

'What does "whatever" mean?'

'Means what it says,' said Bonny. 'Whatever you want. Waiting at the tables, washing up, preparing food, cooking—'

'Cooking?' said Dad.

'Yeah.'

'Are you any good?'

'I'm better than good.'

Maya frowned. There was no doubt that Mum was

35

pressed in the kitchen, but Bonny seemed so unconventional; and there was also the question of the boy in the lane. She studied Dad's face. It was hard to tell whether he was unsettled by the girl or secretly enjoying the challenge of her.

'How old are you?' he said.

'Fifteen.'

'Where do you go to school?'

'It's the summer holidays.'

'I appreciate that,' said Dad, 'but where do you go normally?'

'I'm not that keen on school.'

'I see.' Dad looked her over. 'Where do you live?'

'Round about.'

'What does that mean?'

'It means round about,' said Bonny.

'Have you got any brothers and sisters?'

'No.'

Maya thought of the strange boy again. Bonny glanced quickly at her.

'He's not my brother,' she said.

'Who?' said Dad.

Bonny looked back at him.

'The boy I was with just now.'

'What boy?'

Bonny didn't answer.

'Who is he?' said Maya.

Again no answer.

She looked at Dad. His face was easy to read now. He was going to turn Bonny away; and she didn't blame him. The girl was high risk.

'It's kind of you to come in,' he began, 'and it's true we're going to be taking on some staff fairly soon, but at this precise moment—'

36

A crash cut him short. It came from the direction of the kitchen and there was no mistaking what it was. Somebody—Tom probably—had dropped a pile of crockery. Mum appeared, bustling towards them.

'Maya,' she said breathlessly, 'forget what I said about taking a break. I need you back again.'

'I'll sort it,' said Bonny.

Mum stared at her.

'Who are you?'

'I've come to help out.' Bonny shot a glance at Maya. 'Go to the bench outside the church. Tell Mo—'

'Mo?'

'The big boy you saw. He's called Mo. Tell him Bonny says he's to wait there now till eleven o'clock and then come back. You got that? Tell him nice and firm, and repeat the new time. Do it twice at least. If he gives you a stare, don't worry about it. He does that when he's scared.'

'Scared?'

'He's scared of people,' said Bonny, 'specially adults. Some people freak him so bad he runs away and hides, and I have to go and find him. But he'll be OK with you. Just don't try and make him talk. Give him the message, say it lots of times, and come away.'

Bonny squared up to Dad.

'I'll give you half an hour for free,' she said. 'If I still like you after that, I'll let you pay me.'

And before Dad could answer, she ran off towards the kitchen and disappeared.

'I'll deal with it,' said Mum, hurrying after her.

'And I'll deal with Mo,' said Dad.

'But you'll scare him,' said Maya.

'I don't care,' said Dad. 'I'm not letting you go.'

'I can do it,' she said.

37

She pictured Mo's face: his strange, intense eyes. Maybe Bonny was right: he was scary because he was scared.

'I should do it,' she said. 'I'm not frightening.'

The phone rang. Dad glanced round at it.

'I've got to take that,' he said. 'It's the bank ringing back.'

'I'll speak to Mo,' she said.

'But—'

'I'll be OK,' she said. 'I'm just passing on a message.'

And she stepped outside and set off down the lane. Dad didn't call after her and she was glad of it. She needed to get away from The Rowan Tree. But the relief didn't last long. She felt uneasy the moment she entered the village square.

It wasn't the thought of confronting Mo; it was the sight of the forest just a short distance away. She stopped outside The Rose and Crown and stared through a gap in the houses at the trees beyond.

She would have to face them again soon. She knew that. She'd have to prove to herself that they hadn't beaten her. But not yet. First things first. Find Mo, give him Bonny's instructions, then decide about the forest. She cut down the lane that led to the church, her eyes running ahead to the bench outside the gate.

There was no one sitting there.

She walked up to it and looked round: no one in the lane, no one she could see anyway. She thought of what Bonny had said about Mo running off and hiding if someone scared him badly. She slipped through the gate and gazed round.

Nothing much here, just a small grassy area with a path that led to the entrance of the church. She walked up and tried the door: it was locked. She stepped to the side of the building and peered round into the graveyard.

38

No sign of Mo, just gravestones rising from roughly-mown grass, and beyond the perimeter wall, a patch of bushy ground stretching to the extremity of the forest. She walked further round the church and saw more gravestones over to the left. An air of decay hung upon the place. Then she heard a voice.

'Looking for more bodies, girlie?'

6

She spun round, searching, but there was nobody to be seen. The voice came again.

'Plenty of bodies here. All nice and dead.'

A muscular figure rose from behind one of the larger gravestones: a shaven-headed boy of about nineteen. He was wearing nothing but cut-off shorts and his arms, neck, and chest were heavily tattooed. His eyes were fierce and mocking.

She studied him warily. Mo would definitely have run away from this boy. She checked quickly round. If she started running now, she might just make it to the gate. The boy gave a laugh.

'Yeah, you might get there.'

She looked back at him. He was now sauntering towards her.

'But you might not.' He gave her a wink. 'Go on. Give it a go. I like a challenge.'

She didn't move. She knew there was no point now. He was too close. She faced him, fists clenched. He stopped in front of her and grinned.

'Like what you see, girlie?'

'Not much.'

'Ooh,' he said, 'sparky.'

The tattoos seemed to dance on his body.

'All hunting birds,' he said, surveying them. 'Got 'em on my back too. Come closer if you want to see better.'

She could see them well enough. The most striking one was an owl in the centre of his chest. He moved towards her again. She took a step back. He chuckled.

'Scare easy, don't you?'

She stopped, reluctantly. He stopped too, then leaned closer.

'You're the girl from The Rowan Tree,' he said. 'You're Maya.'

'How do you know?'

'Oh, everyone in Hembury's talking about Maya. Little Maya with the cutie-pie face. The girl who made up the story about the bodies in the forest.'

'I didn't make it up.'

'Don't worry,' said the boy. 'You've got your fantasies. So have I.'

She saw a leer play over his face.

'How come everyone knows about the bodies?' she said.

The boy didn't answer. His eyes were running over her.

'How did the story get out?' she said.

'Who cares?'

'I do.'

He shrugged.

'Probably one of the ambulance men.'

'What do you mean?'

'Sounding off to someone in the village. They get pissed off when they're called out for a hoax.'

'It wasn't a hoax,' she said.

'You reckon?'

The boy leaned closer still.

'Piece of advice,' he whispered. 'Keep away from the forest. Bodies or no bodies, it's a dangerous place. Never know what you might find among the trees.'

She twisted her face away from his. He gave another laugh, then straightened up.

41

'Come and see this,' he said.

And to her surprise, he started back towards the gravestone where she'd first spotted him. She looked over at the lane. If she made a dash now, she might just get away. The boy was still striding on. But he called over his shoulder.

'I'd still catch you.'

She caught the taunt in his voice and walked after him. He'd reached the gravestone now and was bent over something she couldn't make out.

'Get a load of this,' he said.

She walked closer.

'If you've got the bottle,' he added.

'What do you want to show me?' she said, as confidently as she could.

But she could see now. Lying on the grass was a dead fox, or part of a dead fox. There was no head. The stomach had been slit open and the entrails strewn about. The corpse reeked. She started to gag and turned aside.

'Head gone, heart cut out,' said the boy matter-of-factly. 'Same as the others.'

'What others?'

She forced herself to turn back. The boy seemed unmoved by the fox. He was staring down at the carcass, but he didn't seem to care much about it.

'What others?' she said.

'Oh, there's others,' he murmured. 'Just like this bastard. And you know what's weird?'

He looked round at her.

'It only started happening after you and your family moved into the village.'

'But we didn't have anything to do with this,' she said.

The boy didn't answer. He was studying the fox again.

'See the legs?' he said after a moment. 'Got himself caught in a trap, this one. You can see from the way they're mangled up. He hurt 'em trying to pull himself free. But it wasn't the trap that killed him. He was alive when he got ripped up.'

The boy stood up, stepped over to the next gravestone and picked up a large canvas bag she hadn't noticed. Then he walked back, seized the dead fox and pushed the bloody corpse into it.

'Are you going to take the fox away?' she said.

'Why? Do you want it?'

She stared at the bag. The boy had left it open and she could see the fox's mutilated form inside. It was twisted in such a way that the dead face would have stared out at her, had it been there.

She remembered the yellow eyes she'd seen and wondered whether this was the same animal. She let her gaze move on. It caught other things inside the bag: a half-eaten apple, a beanie, an empty knife sheath. She looked quickly back at the boy.

'It's not on me,' he said, watching her.

'What isn't?'

'The thing you're freaking your head over.'

The boy's eyes were mocking her again.

'See?' he said. 'Nothing in my pockets.'

He pulled them out—empty.

'But maybe,' he said, 'hmm, yeah, let me think. Maybe I left it somewhere.'

He looked elaborately round.

'Ah, there it is.'

And he reached down to another thing she hadn't noticed.

A knife stuck in the grass.

'Must have fallen out of my hand,' he muttered, 'and

43

then stuck in the ground all by itself. Funny how that happened, eh?'

She yearned to run now, but she knew it was pointless. He'd catch her within seconds. The boy straightened up, turning the blade in his hand, then he looked at her.

'It's how things are, girlie.'

His voice had hardened. She didn't move.

'You're pathetic,' he went on. 'You know that? You people from the outside. Townies, whatever, you're all the same. You see a dead animal and you go to pieces. But it's how things are. Law of the jungle. Kill or be killed. Ask no quarter, give none. And you know what?'

He took a step towards her.

'Foxy doesn't mind this. He knows how it is. Sometimes you get lucky, sometimes you get caught. Do you think he's any less ruthless? He doesn't just kill to eat. He kills when you're on his patch. He kills when you're after his mate or his young. And sometimes he kills just because he wants to.'

She caught a shadow in the corner of her eye, someone moving in the lane. She thought of Mo, but prayed it was Dad. The boy glanced towards it, then at the knife, then at her.

'Nature's code,' he said. 'All animals accept it. Except humans.'

And he picked up the bag, slung it over his shoulder and set off towards the low wall at the far end of the graveyard. She watched, trembling, but he didn't look back. He clambered over the wall and strode off over the bushy ground towards the forest.

She stumbled round to the front of the church, desperate to get back to The Rowan Tree. The figure she'd sensed earlier was a woman about Mum's age, walking towards the gate. She saw Maya and called out.

44

'Are you all right?'

The voice sounded imperious. Maya stopped.

'Are you all right?' called the woman again.

Maya looked at her. An elegant face, slightly haughty, and something in it made her feel she was more of an inconvenience than a concern.

'I'm fine,' she answered.

She walked through the gate and out into the lane.

'What's happened?' said the woman.

Maya darted a look in the direction of the graveyard.

'I came here looking for Mo,' she said. 'Bonny's friend.'

The woman said nothing.

'And there was this boy,' she went on. 'He was shaven-headed—'

'With tattoos,' said the woman.

'Yes. Do you know him?'

'Where is he now?' said the woman, glancing round.

'He walked off towards the forest.'

The woman stared in that direction for a few moments, then looked back at her.

'I'd keep away from him, if I were you,' she said.

'Who is he?'

'He's called Zep.'

'Does he live here?'

'He lives all over the place. This village, other villages, God knows where else. He turns up, disappears, turns up again. He's a law unto himself.'

The woman glanced towards the forest again, then back.

'I'll walk with you to The Rowan Tree,' she said.

'How do you know I'm from there?' said Maya.

But she already knew what was coming.

'You're Maya Munro,' said the woman. 'You're the girl who—'

'Made up the story about the bodies,' said Maya.

The woman looked her over.

'And did you?'

'No,' said Maya.

They started walking back down the lane, but almost at once a new figure appeared. It was Bonny, sprinting towards them from the square. The girl took no notice of the woman and headed straight for Maya.

'Where's Mo?' she demanded.

'I couldn't find him.'

'So why didn't you come and get me?'

'I tried looking for him,' said Maya. 'I went in the grave-yard and—'

'Yeah? And what?'

'Maya's a little shaken,' said the woman.

'Who's asking you?' said Bonny.

'She's had an encounter with Zep.'

'Zep was in there?'

'Yes,' said the woman.

'Christ's sake!' Bonny glared at Maya. 'I knew there was something wrong when you didn't come back. You should have bloody got me!'

And before Maya could answer, Bonny tore down the lane, burst through the gate into the churchyard and disappeared from view. Maya stared after her.

'Don't worry about Bonny,' said the woman. 'She's always been rude.'

'She doesn't like you much,' said Maya.

'I don't like her much either,' said the woman. 'Or her big, bumbling friend.'

'Where do they live?'

'On a smallholding near the edge of the village. A rather disreputable old woman called Granny owns it. She's always had an open door to vagrants and riff-raff.

Bonny and Mo turned up in the village a year or so ago, and they've dossed in Granny's outhouse ever since, I'm afraid. I think Social Services have tried to intervene, but to no avail.'

'Where did they come from before that?'

'I don't know and I don't care,' said the woman.

They walked on, into the square, past The Rose and Crown, up the lane towards The Rowan Tree. The woman had fallen silent and her face seemed severe. Then suddenly she spoke.

'Be careful, Maya.'

'Careful of what?'

They reached the door of The Rowan Tree and stopped.

'Just be careful,' said the woman. 'All right?'

She held out a hand.

'Rebecca Flint.'

Maya took it.

'Thank you for walking back with me,' she said. 'Do you . . . do you want to come in and have a coffee or something?'

To her relief, Rebecca Flint shook her head.

'I haven't been inside The Rowan Tree for months,' she said, 'and I don't intend to do so now. Or ever again.'

Maya stared at her.

'But why?'

Rebecca Flint turned away.

'It was nice to meet you,' she said.

7

Maya walked in through the front door. Mum and Dad were in the office, their backs to her. Mum was on the phone, Dad beside her, and neither appeared to have seen her come in. Tom came hurrying up.

'Sis, you were ages. You OK?'

'I've been better,' she said.

She nodded towards the office.

'What's going on in there?'

'Money.'

'Are they still talking to the bank?'

'No,' said Tom, 'but it's about money.'

He steered her away to the lounge. The elderly couple from Room Five were sitting there, reading. The man looked up.

'Anything I can get you, Mr Adams?' said Tom.

'I'm fine, thank you.'

'Mrs Adams?'

'I'm fine too.' The woman smiled. 'But thank you for asking.'

Tom eased Maya back into the corridor.

'Kitchen?' he said.

'Yeah.'

They made their way to the kitchen and sat down at the table.

'What's going on?' said Maya.

'The bank's getting rough.'

'Why?'

'Dad won't say. Or Mum. They just keep telling me everything'll be OK once The Rowan Tree starts making money. But I think we're struggling to make the repayments.'

'So who's Mum speaking to on the phone?'

'Remember her friend Caroline?' said Tom.

'No.'

'Yes, you do. We met her in London.'

'The music business,' said Maya.

'That's right. Well, she's kind of loaded and I think Mum's asking her for help. Just to tide us over.'

'Christ.'

'So if Mum and Dad are a bit tetchy,' said Tom, 'it's because they've got a lot on their minds.'

Maya looked down.

'Yeah, I know,' said Tom. 'You've got a lot on your mind too.'

He paused.

'You don't look great, sis.'

'Thanks.'

'You look shaken again.'

'I feel shaken.'

'Did you find Mo?'

'No.'

'So what happened?'

She told him about Zep, the knife, the mutilated fox.

'Bloody hell,' said Tom. 'You should have told me that straight away. Do you think we ought to call the police?'

'They're not going to believe anything I say, are they?'

'Even so.'

'There's no point,' she said. 'I didn't get hurt or anything. And they must know about Zep already. Listen, there's something else. I met this woman.'

She described the meeting with Rebecca Flint, and the walk home.

'Just as well she turned up,' said Tom. 'Was Bonny really rude to her?'

'Yes,' said Maya, 'and to me.'

'Mum and Dad won't be taking her on.'

'What was she like here?' said Maya.

'Brilliant.'

'You kidding?'

'No,' said Tom, 'she was amazing. She's a force of nature. She just took over. Cleared up the plates I smashed, helped Mum in the kitchen, whizzed round the dining room, chatting away to people. She even had that grumpy guy from Table Six smiling. But then it was like Cinderella.'

'What do you mean?' said Maya.

'Like she suddenly remembered the time. She was clearing Table Two, then she just looked at her watch, asked me if you'd come back, and when I said no, she ran off. Not a word, nothing. I think her whole world revolves round this Mo character.'

Maya leaned back in the chair, trying to think, trying to calm down. From the lane came the clip-clop of horses passing by, then silence fell once more. Nothing in The Rowan Tree seemed to break it.

'I wish you were happy, sis,' said Tom.

She looked at him.

'What's wrong?' he said. 'I don't just mean the stuff with Zep and Bonny. I mean, what's really wrong?'

'Something here,' she answered. 'At The Rowan Tree.'

'But it's a beautiful old place,' said Tom. 'I love it. So do Mum and Dad.'

'Something's wrong here,' she said. 'That woman knows it too.'

'Rebecca Flint?'

50

'Yes,' said Maya. 'I offered her a coffee and she said she hadn't been inside The Rowan Tree for months, and had no intention of coming in again, ever. And she wouldn't explain why.'

Tom laughed.

'She probably came for a meal here and the chef had a bad day.'

'It's more than that,' said Maya. 'It's something else.' She hesitated. 'I heard scratching last night. When I was in my room. Everything was quiet and then I heard this . . . scratching sound. Just a few times. Then silence.'

Tom said nothing.

And she knew what that meant.

She stood up and walked over to the window. Through it she could see Mr and Mrs Adams walking down the lane towards the square. They were holding hands. She followed them with her eyes until they disappeared inside The Rose and Crown.

'Sis?' said Tom.

She looked round at him.

'It's not The Rowan Tree that's the problem,' he said. 'It's the forest. That's what's really spooking you. You ought to go back there, you know? Not on your own, I don't mean. I'd come with you. But you ought to face it again. We could go to that clearing together. Where you had that nasty experience.'

'You mean the bodies I didn't see?'

'Whatever,' said Tom. 'But we ought to go there. You might feel better if you've stared the place down. We could go now if you want. Mum and Dad said I could take a break.'

She glanced out of the window again. Tom was right; she knew that. She ought to face the forest again. She even wanted to. But not yet. There was something else she had to confront first; something far closer.

'No, thanks, Tommy.'

She turned towards the door.

'Sis, you look really weird.'

'What do you mean?'

'Like that time on the path. Before you ran off.'

She heard the fear in his voice.

'I'm not going to run off,' she said.

She forced a smile.

'I'm just going to my room.'

She started towards the door. She had to check the pendant, reassure herself once again that she hadn't imagined everything; and she had to pretend that she wasn't frightened of her own room.

'I'll see you later,' she said.

'That policewoman turned up,' said Tom.

She stopped.

'WPC Shaw,' he said.

'What did she want?'

'She was only here about a minute,' said Tom. 'Said she's lost a horseshoe pendant and thinks she might have dropped it here. Asked us to keep an eye out for it. Maybe that's what she was looking for when I saw her turning stuff over in the reception area.' He sniffed. 'I still don't like her.'

Maya hurried out of the kitchen and down the corridor towards the stairs. Mum and Dad were still busy in the office and neither glanced in her direction as she slipped past. She made her way to the first floor and down to her room.

The door faced her.

She stared at it, her mind on the horseshoe pendant hidden just beyond. She pictured it glinting in the forest as it dangled from Annie Shaw's neck. Perhaps it was glinting now beneath the floorboard. She reached out to open the door, then pulled her hand back, and on an impulse scraped a fingernail down the wood.

Scratch.

She did it again.

Scratch, scratch.

She pushed open the door, stepped in and closed it behind her. The room was exactly as she'd left it, but a heavy stillness hung there. She walked over to the bed and stopped, listening, looking round; then she reached down, pulled back the carpet and prised up the floorboard just enough to make space for her hand. No need to pull the whole thing up. She knew where the pendant was. She squeezed her hand through and felt for it.

Nothing.

She stopped, her hand still hidden in the dark space below the floorboard. This couldn't be right. This was exactly the place where she'd dropped the pendant. She started to feel round again. Nothing as before.

She felt a growing unease. She stretched herself out over the floor, pushed her hand in at a different angle, and started to feel further under the board. Still nothing. She drew her arm slowly back towards the gap, and as she did so, something brushed her hand.

What it was she didn't know.

She only knew that it wasn't the pendant.

She felt round the object with her fingers. Something small, something hard, and then—

'Ah!'

Something sharp. It had pricked her thumb. She dropped the object and pulled her hand out. She was breathing fast. She stared down at the gap. There was only one thing for it.

She pulled the carpet right back, then eased the board

up higher until she could see all the way into the space beneath. There was only one thing lying between the joists, and it wasn't Annie Shaw's pendant.

It was a carved wooden effigy about four inches long. Male or female, she couldn't tell. All that was certain was that it had two legs, two arms, and no head. Where the head should have been, there was only the point of a long nail that had been driven through the figure from between the legs, impaling it.

'Oh, God,' she murmured.

The floorboard slid from her grasp and slammed back. She looked about her, panic starting. The carpet was slowly rolling back by itself. She reached out, caught it, jerked it back, yanked up the floorboard, stared at the effigy; then pulled it out and dropped it on the carpet.

'Horrible, horrible,' she muttered.

The effigy seemed to stare up at her, even without a face.

'I'm not having you in my room,' she said.

She picked it up, ran to the window, opened it and made ready to throw the effigy as far as she could—then stopped. Below her was the path round the side of The Rowan Tree, the garage, the bins, the oil tank and beyond the boundary wall the front garden of next door. She couldn't throw the thing out here.

It had to go where it would never be found.

She stared towards the forest. It was the obvious place and she needn't go far in. The trees just up from the graveyard were tightly packed and there were bushes and thickets too. She saw a figure moving among them and thought of Zep.

But it was not Zep.

It was a man with red hair.

She watched, tensely. Even from this distance, she

recognized him. She made up her mind, thrust the effigy in her pocket and tore downstairs. Mum and Dad had left the office, but she could hear their voices in the lounge, together with others she didn't know. She ran on past and burst into the kitchen.

Tom was sitting at the table, making a sandwich.

'Not now, Tommy,' she said.

'But—'

'Bring it with you.'

She took him by the hand.

'We're going to the forest.'

8

'I thought you wanted to find that clearing,' said Tom.

Maya looked around her. Before them was a small glade and the track they'd been following cut straight through it. But it also split left and right.

'It's got to be somewhere to the left,' said Tom. 'That's nearer to where Dad found you.'

She turned right: the red-haired man had definitely been walking in that direction.

'Sis,' said Tom, 'the clearing won't be this way.'

She carried on walking.

'Sis!'

She stopped and looked at him.

'What's going on?' he said. 'You're acting strange. And you've still got that weird face.'

'I didn't know.'

'And you're not saying anything.'

'Sorry.'

'So what's this about?' he said. 'First you don't want to go to the forest and then you do. Then you don't want to go and find the clearing. You just walk off in the other direction. And you keep looking round all the time, like you're searching for something.'

She glanced round again, unable to stop herself. She felt guilty about Tom, but she knew she couldn't tell him about the red-haired man or the effigy in her pocket. He'd disbelieve in the first and freak out over the second.

There'd been no further glimpses of the red-haired man.

But here at least was something promising. A dense clump of bushes just down from the track. It would do perfectly for one of her reasons for being here. The problem was how to distract Tom. Fortunately he managed this by himself.

'That's a jay,' he said. 'Hear it? Over there. It's somewhere in that glade.'

And he wandered back to look. As he did so, she pulled the effigy from her pocket, flung it into the bushes and whipped round to face him again. He was still peering into the glade.

'Can't see it,' he said, 'but I definitely heard a jay.'

He turned back towards her and she saw his face darken.

'Who the hell's that?' he said.

He was staring past her shoulder. She spun round and to her horror saw Zep climbing to his feet from among the bushes where she'd just thrown the effigy. He seemed even wilder than in the graveyard. Not only was he covered in earth and leaves but the cut-off shorts were gone and he was completely naked.

There was no sign of the effigy.

She felt Tom draw close.

'I presume that's Zep,' he murmured.

'Yes.'

She went on staring at the boy, but now a second figure was stirring from the bushes: a girl about fifteen. She had black hair and was wearing nothing save a long, loose shirt, which she was casually buttoning up.

'It's Bonny,' whispered Tom.

The girl stood up and shook her hair.

'No, it's not,' said Maya.

'You're right.'

The girl stood next to Zep and watched them for a moment in silence, then, with the same casual air, she reached down, pulled on some jeans, and without a backward glance either at them or at Zep, she sloped off and disappeared among the trees.

Zep took no notice of her at all.

His eyes were on Maya.

'I don't like the way that boy's looking at you,' said Tom. 'Shit, he's coming over.'

Zep was striding across, still naked.

'Stay back!' shouted Tom. 'And put some clothes on!'

Zep came on, loose and muscular, the tattoos moving on his body. The familiar leer played round his mouth. Tom pulled Maya behind him.

'Stay back!' he called.

'Or what, pygmy?'

'Tommy,' said Maya. 'Come on, let's go. You can't fight him.'

Tom ignored her.

'Tommy,' she urged him, 'come on!'

'Tommy,' mimicked Zep, 'come on!'

'Shut your mouth!' said Tom.

'Shut your mouth!' mimicked Zep.

The boy stopped in front of them. Tom squared up to him.

'Tommy,' said Maya.

'Stay out of it, sis.'

She stepped in front of him and scowled up at Zep.

'Leave us alone, Zep,' she said.

The boy raised an eyebrow.

'Found out my name, have you? Does that mean you like me?' He gave her a wink. 'Keep your eyes on my face, cutie-pie. Don't let 'em drop. Or you might see something scary. Know what I mean? Unless . . . that's what you really want.'

He started to edge closer.

'Who's killing the foxes?' she said hurriedly.

He stopped, still watching her.

'Who's killing the foxes?' she said. 'And mutilating them?'

She didn't suppose he'd answer this. But it might stave off trouble to keep him talking.

'Who's doing it?'

Zep stayed close, his eyes moving over her.

'Who's doing it?' he murmured. 'You really want to know?'

He chuckled.

'Gather round, children. Listen to Uncle Zep.'

Maya felt Tom's arms lock round her from behind. Zep gave a slow grin.

'Did you know,' he said, 'that in some parts of the world, they reckon if you eat the brain of an animal, you capture its cunning. And if you eat the heart, you capture its strength.' He paused. 'Works for humans too.'

'What's your point?' said Tom.

'Just that there's bad magic going on, pygmy. That's why I warned little Maya to keep away from the forest. But it seems she just can't do it.' He looked at Maya and mouthed a kiss. 'Can you, baby?'

'So who's behind this?' she said.

'Come with me.'

And Zep set off towards the glade where Tom had heard the jay.

'Let's get out of here,' whispered Tom.

Zep called over his shoulder.

'Come on, little Maya.'

'Let's go,' said Tom.

'Come on, baby,' called Zep. 'You liked the last thing I showed you.'

Maya set off after Zep. Tom caught her by the arm.

'What are you doing?' he muttered.

'Showing him we're not scared.'

'But it's going to be another fox with its head cut off.'

'I don't care,' she said. 'We've got to stand up to him.'

'This is stupid.'

She entered the glade. Zep had already crossed it and was walking into the close-packed trees on the far side. He moved confidently, even as the foliage folded around him; and then he was gone.

'Sis,' said Tom, 'let's go.'

'Wait.'

Something was stirring in the leaves ahead, and it wasn't Zep. She stared at the foliage. All was still once more; then she caught it again: a clear movement. She thought of the red-haired man, but instead caught a flash of yellow.

Quickly gone.

She peered ahead, searching. Nothing at first, just static branches, static leaves, then she saw them again: two yellow eyes, staring towards her. They were further back now, deeper among the trees and almost invisible, but they were clearly watching her.

She felt certain this was the fox she'd seen yesterday.

'Sis,' said Tom, 'what are you looking at?'

'Can't you see them?'

'See what?'

She started to walk towards the eyes.

'Sis,' said Tom, 'don't go that way.'

'I want to.'

'But it's the way Zep just went.'

'I told you. We've got to show him we're not scared.'

She walked on, through the trees and on towards the spot where she'd seen the yellow eyes. They'd vanished once more, but here was Zep again. He was standing over to the right by a huge horse-chestnut tree. The bark on the side facing them had been savagely cut back to form a shape in the tree-trunk as broad and tall as Zep himself.

And identical to the headless effigy.

She saw Zep catch sight of her and smirk. Tom tugged at her wrist, but she resisted.

'That's right,' called Zep. 'Don't let him pull you away.'

'Shut your mouth!' shouted Tom.

'Ah, bless!'

'You bastard!'

Tom started forward. Maya caught him by the arm.

'Don't, Tommy.'

Zep laughed, then turned his naked body fully round towards them, and gave a whoop.

'Come on, children! No need to be embarrassed. It's all fun in Uncle Zep's Garden of Eden.'

And still facing them, he stepped back against the tree and into the shape that had been carved there. It was almost a perfect fit. Except for the obvious thing.

'Shame about the missing head,' he said, looking at Maya. 'Maybe I should cut mine off, then I can stand here nice and snug. What do you reckon, cutie-pie?'

She didn't answer. Zep smirked again, then suddenly turned his head and stared behind him. Maya looked in the same direction, but all she saw was trees. Zep turned back and met her eyes again.

'Things to do,' he said.

And he sprinted straight at them.

'Maya,' said Tom, 'get behind me.'

She stayed where she was, still gripping Tom's arm. Tom pushed her hand away and stepped in front of her. Zep thundered towards them, a look of wild exhilaration on his face. As he drew close, he gave a shout.

61

'Hey!'

Tom raised his fists.

'Come on, Tommy!' shouted Zep.

Tom took a step forward—but there was to be no fight. With a crazed laugh, Zep raced past, burst through the trees behind them, and disappeared. Tom ran after him.

'Tommy!' called Maya.

'I'm just checking,' he answered, and disappeared too.

Maya stared nervously after him, but he was soon back.

'Are you all right?' she said.

'Yeah.'

'What happened?'

'He made for those bushes,' said Tom. 'Where we saw him with that girl.'

'Then what?'

'Just picked up his shorts and walked off.'

'Did he see you watching him?'

'Don't know. He's gone anyway.' Tom looked round. 'I wonder what made him run.'

But Maya had seen the answer. Two men were walking towards them from beyond the horse-chestnut tree. One was about fifty, tough and capable-looking, but she was only interested in his companion: a man of about thirty-five with an unmistakable face.

And unmistakable red hair.

9

She watched. There was no question that this was the man she'd seen lying on the forest floor. The sight of him moving filled her with a sick fear. He couldn't, he shouldn't be walking. It was as unnatural as Annie Shaw being alive.

Yet the figure approaching her looked vigorous and strong. He walked with a light step, his arms swinging freely, hands easing aside the foliage that blocked his way: a ghost that had somehow returned to its body.

The men drew close and stopped. Neither was smiling.

'Hello,' said Maya.

The older man looked her over with obvious disapproval.

'Maya Munro,' he growled.

'Yes,' she said. 'This is my brother Tom.'

'I know who he is.'

'How come?' said Tom.

The man grunted.

'There aren't many secrets in Hembury,' he said. 'Pick your nose at one end of the village and they'll know about it five minutes later at the other. I know exactly who you two are, and frankly I could do without bumping into either of you, especially young Maya.'

'That's friendly,' said Tom.

'I don't feel friendly towards girls who waste other people's time with stories about non-existent dead bodies.'

'Maya didn't—'

'Oh, get real,' said the man. 'You want to stick up for your sister, good for you. But make sure you know the facts. Because she's probably not telling you the truth either.'

The man turned to Maya.

'You wasted a lot of people's time. Police, ambulance crew, God knows who else. And you wasted our time.' He glanced at his companion. 'A lot of our time.'

'Who are you?' said Maya.

'McMurdo,' came the answer. 'I'm the forester in charge here. This is Bryn, my assistant.'

Maya looked warily at the red-haired man.

'You don't have to be rude,' said Tom.

'I speak as I find,' said McMurdo, 'and I don't much care whether you like it or not. This is our patch and as you can see . . . '

His eye fell on the damaged horse-chestnut.

'We've got enough trouble to deal with already without Maya adding to it.'

Maya forced herself to look at Bryn again. He was watching her with the same grave expression he'd had from the start, though whether he shared McMurdo's disapproval of her she couldn't tell.

'Who's damaging the trees?' she said.

Neither man answered.

'Who's killing the foxes?'

McMurdo looked back at her.

'You know about them, do you?'

'Who's doing it?' she said. 'You must know. You just said there aren't any secrets in Hembury.'

'I said there aren't many,' said McMurdo. 'I didn't say there aren't any.'

'So do you know who's doing this?'

McMurdo said nothing.

'Is it Zep?' she said.

She looked at Bryn again. He still hadn't spoken and she found she wanted him to. She didn't know why. But McMurdo cut in again.

'You've met Zep, have you?'

'I met him in the graveyard this morning. He was standing over a dead fox.'

She told the men what had happened.

'Carried it off, did he?' said McMurdo.

'Yes. He said there are lots of dead foxes turning up. Is that true?'

'It might be.'

'We just saw Zep again,' said Tom.

'Where?' said McMurdo.

'Here in the forest. He was with a girl in the bushes.'

'He's always with some girl,' said the forester. 'They can't keep off him. Don't ask me why.'

'This one just walked off.'

'Sensible kid.'

'But Zep hung around. He had no clothes on.'

'Oh, Jesus.' McMurdo glanced at Bryn. 'Not again.'

'He threatened us a bit,' said Tom, 'but he ran off when he saw you two coming.'

'I bet he did.'

'You haven't answered my question,' said Maya.

'Oh, really?' said McMurdo.

'Yes, really,' she said.

The forester's eye hardened.

'And what question would that be?'

'Is Zep behind the dead foxes?' she said. 'And the damaged trees?'

Again she wished Bryn would answer; but again McMurdo did so.

'We don't know who's behind it,' he said.

'So it could be Zep?' said Tom.

'Could easily be Zep,' said McMurdo. 'He's wild enough to do anything. But it could easily be someone else. Zep's not the only crazy individual round here. It's someone twisted, whoever it is.'

The forester's gaze moved left and right. Maya looked at Bryn again; and this time he spoke.

'The police came to see me.'

'What's that got to do with us?' said Tom.

'I'm talking to Maya.'

'What's it got to do with her?'

Bryn glanced at him.

'You do all the talking for your sister, do you?'

'When she wants me to.'

'And she wants you to now, does she?'

'Yes,' said Tom.

'Have you asked her?'

'I don't need to. I just know.'

'Tommy,' said Maya, 'it's OK.'

Bryn looked at her.

'The police came to see me,' he said. 'Told me the new girl at The Rowan Tree had got herself lost in the forest and reported seeing some bodies lying dead, including a red-haired man of about thirty-five.'

'So?' said Tom.

'Christ, boy,' said Bryn, 'you really are a work of art. I wish I'd had a brother as bolshie as you. I only want to ask your sister a question.'

'Tommy,' said Maya, 'let it go.'

She looked at Bryn.

'What do you want to ask me?' she said.

But she already knew.

'They came to see me,' said Bryn, 'because there aren't that many red-haired men of about thirty-five round

66

these parts. And none in Hembury, apart from me.'

He paused.

'I was obviously able to tell them it wasn't me. Firstly, I'm not dead—as you might have noticed—and secondly, I was in The Rose and Crown when you were supposed to be in the forest.'

'Supposed?' said Tom.

'All right,' said Bryn. 'I was in The Rose and Crown when your sister was in the forest, OK? But, Maya, can you tell me—what did this red-haired man look like?'

'He looked like you,' she said.

Bryn shifted on his feet.

'Like me?'

'Yes.'

'How like me?'

Maya hesitated.

'Very like you,' she said.

McMurdo snorted.

'Still making things up, young lady?'

'I'm not,' she said.

'Come on, Bryn,' said the forester. 'Let's go.'

'Wait,' said Bryn. 'What was he wearing, Maya? This red-haired man.'

She looked down.

'A suit, tie, white shirt, and . . .'

'And what?'

'He had a silver watch.'

'I haven't got a silver watch,' said Bryn.

She heard the relief in his voice.

'You were in The Rose and Crown,' she said quietly.

From somewhere nearby came the flapping of wings—then a crash in the undergrowth. Maya looked up again and saw both men peering round, Tom too. She searched the trees on either side. Nothing suspicious.

Another crash in the undergrowth, panting, footsteps. Someone running away, over to the left.

'There!' said McMurdo.

'Got it,' said Bryn.

The figure disappeared in the trees.

'See who it was?' said McMurdo.

'Yep.'

'So did I. Let's go.'

McMurdo glared at Maya and Tom.

'You two, get back to The Rowan Tree. Stay away from the forest till this stuff gets sorted out. And you, young lady—no more fantasy stories.'

And the forester set off at a run. Bryn lingered.

'Know the way back?'

'Course we do,' said Tom.

Bryn pointed.

'Cut through those trees. Keep walking straight and you'll pick up a track that takes you to the top of the graveyard.'

And he raced after McMurdo.

'Tommy,' said Maya, 'did you see who that figure was?'

'I didn't even see a figure.'

'It was Bonny. I saw her clearly.'

'Then Mo must be somewhere that way. She'll be running towards him.'

Maya stared after the two men. Both had now disappeared and silence had returned to the forest. She looked the other way. Bryn's directions were simple enough, yet something felt wrong. Something to do with Bonny.

'She's not running towards Mo,' she murmured.

'What do you mean, sis?'

She started to walk the way Bryn had pointed. Tom caught her up.

'What do you mean?' he said.

'I don't know. I just . . . '

She kept walking, through stands of young birch and on into a small glade—and then she stopped.

'Now what?' said Tom.

'Bonny's not running towards Mo. She's running in the opposite direction.'

'What for?'

'To lead those men away from him.'

'What are you talking about?'

Maya nodded to the far side of the glade.

'Christ,' said Tom.

Three of the trees had headless images carved from their bark. At the base of one was the corpse of another fox, head gone, stomach slit open. Mo was bent over it, his back to them.

'Christ,' said Tom again.

Mo whirled round, saw them and jumped to his feet. His shirt, trousers, and arms were covered with blood.

'Easy, Mo,' called Maya. 'We're friends.'

'No, we're not,' muttered Tom.

The boy stared at them with savage eyes.

'That's fox's blood on him,' said Tom. 'It's got to be.'

'Easy, Mo,' said Maya. 'It's OK.'

She heard running steps behind them, then McMurdo's voice.

'Leave the fox, Mo. Leave it where it is.'

Mo bent down and seized the corpse.

'Sis,' said Tom. 'See that?'

But she'd already spotted the severed head of the fox, dropped among the entrails. Mo picked it up and clutched it to his chest, together with the rest of the corpse.

'Leave it!' roared McMurdo.

But Mo was running. He'd tightened his grip on the

corpse and the severed head and was racing with them into the trees. A moment later he was gone. McMurdo and Bryn thundered after him and vanished too. Maya stared after them, then turned and looked around her.

There was no sign of Bonny.

10

Another night, another wait: for sleep, or whatever else might come. She no longer knew what to expect. She stared up at the ceiling. At least she wasn't pacing the floor this time, but she wasn't in bed either. She was lying on it, still in her day-clothes; and she was more frightened than ever.

She turned her head, stared down at the carpet, pictured the floorboard underneath, and the space beneath that; and then the effigy, the images cut into the trees, the fox's corpse. Mo's face as he ran away.

Half past midnight.

One o'clock.

Half past.

She thought back over all that had happened. She didn't suppose Dad's call to the police would have had much effect. They'd surely be keeping an eye on Zep already, and as for the incident with Mo, McMurdo or Bryn would have reported that.

Dad needn't have bothered ringing. No one would care what the girl from The Rowan Tree said.

She sat up, switched on the light.

The blackness scattered but something of it stayed in the air. She stared round the room. It felt like a tomb. She listened for her own breathing and found she could not hear it. She stood up, slipped out of her clothes and put on her nightie, then climbed into bed.

She felt no better. She pulled the duvet up to her chin and peered over the top. Everything she saw seemed somehow menacing. She knew this was foolish. Most of the things in this room she'd brought with her from London: the bed, the desk, the wardrobe, the smaller items of furniture, and all her possessions.

Yet here, in this strange new place, it was as though they'd changed their character; as though they belonged to someone else. Like the room itself. She thought of the space under the floorboard again.

Two o'clock.

'Sleep,' she muttered, and turned off the light.

As she did so, something broke the silence.

She sat up. She'd definitely heard a creak somewhere near. She listened for it again—nothing. She frowned. It might be perfectly normal. But every sound felt hostile now; and the silence even more.

Another creak, then a new noise, something she couldn't place. It was somewhere above her, off to the right. She climbed out of bed and stood there in the darkness. But the sounds had stopped again.

She tried to think. The guest bedrooms were mostly on the ground and first floors but there was one on the second floor, and Mr and Mrs Martin were in there. It could be one of them moving about. Or there was the attic room at the very top of the hotel.

But nobody would be up there. The noise came again, closer, softer, then silence fell once more. A long silence. She slumped in the chair, listening. The silence went on, on.

Half past two.

Quarter to three.

Footsteps in the lane below.

She hurried to the window, eased back the curtain and

stared down. Nobody moving in the lane. She searched for shadows in the gaps between cottages, but there was no sign of a figure.

The footsteps came again, off to the left, as though someone were padding round the side of The Rowan Tree. She slipped over to the other window, eased back the curtain and peered out. Still nobody.

Just darkness and silence.

She sat back in the chair, trembling.

Three o'clock.

Half past.

A sound in the corridor.

Shuffling.

She clutched the sides of the chair, but all was quiet again. She thought of Tom. He'd crept here last night to see her. It might be him out in the corridor. Then she heard it, on the door of her room. The sound she dreaded.

Scratch, scratch, scratch.

She pressed her hands to her ears and screamed.

What happened next was a blur. She remembered the screams going on and on, then somehow she was curled up on her bed, and Mum was holding her, and Tom was standing by, and she was sobbing. From outside in the corridor came the sound of Dad reassuring guests.

'A nightmare,' he was saying. 'She gets them some-times. It's just one of those things.'

'Nightmare,' she murmured.

She stared into Mum's face. But it was Tom who spoke.

'What happened, sis? Was it really a nightmare?'

She heard the voices outside recede as the guests moved off down the corridor. A moment later Dad slipped into the room, closed the door behind him and hurried over.

'Sweetheart,' he said.

She looked back at Tom.

'It wasn't a nightmare,' she said. 'I heard these sounds. Creaking and shuffling, and then . . . scratching at the door. Like last night.'

'You told me about the scratching,' he said. 'When we were talking in the kitchen.'

'You didn't believe me.'

'I never said that.'

'You didn't anyway. You probably still don't.'

She saw Mum and Dad exchange glances.

'You never told us about the scratching,' said Dad.

'I didn't think you'd believe me either.'

'Maya—'

'I heard it,' she said. 'On the outside of the door. And I heard footsteps too. Out in the lane. Heading round the side of the building. Towards the back garden.'

'I'll check it out,' said Dad. He stroked her face. 'It's probably nothing to worry about. I know it's the early hours but somebody might have been wandering around. Doesn't mean it's anyone dangerous.'

He kissed her.

'I'm sorry,' she said.

'There's nothing to be sorry about.'

'I'm being weak.'

'No, you're not,' said Dad.

'Maya,' said Mum, 'you're frightened. That's what you are. And it's understandable. You had a really nasty experience in the forest yesterday, enough to freak anyone out, then another nasty experience in the graveyard with Zep, and yet another one with Mo and the fox. No wonder you're jumping at every sound.'

Mum took her hand.

'And that's understandable too,' she said. 'Old houses can be creepy. No question about it. They make all kinds

74

of noises. My aunt Muriel had an old house in Suffolk and I stayed there when I was a girl. Didn't sleep a wink. I kept thinking I could hear footsteps and tapping noises and goodness knows what. There was nobody else there, of course, just me and Aunt Muriel. But it sounded like the place was full of people wandering about.'

Maya said nothing. Tom yawned.

'Back to bed,' said Dad. 'Come on. All of us.'

'Let's go, Maya,' said Mum.

'What do you mean?' said Maya.

'You're sleeping with me. In our room.'

'But what about Dad?'

'Don't worry about me,' said Dad. 'I'll make up a bed in one of the empty guest rooms.'

'Sorry, Dad,' she said.

'Stop saying sorry,' he said. 'I'll be OK. But I'm just going to check outside first. Make sure there's no one hanging around.'

'Do you have to go out?' said Maya.

'I'll be fine,' said Dad.

He kissed her again.

'Get some sleep, OK? And try not to worry. We'll come through this.'

And without another word, he turned and left them.

'Come on, Maya,' said Mum. 'No arguments.'

Maya had no intention of arguing. She couldn't wait to curl up with Mum in the big bed. Tom returned to his own room and she and Mum made their way to the main bedroom.

'Now then,' said Mum, closing the door behind them. 'Let's get you off to sleep.'

From outside The Rowan Tree came the sound of footsteps.

'Come on, sweetie,' said Mum. 'Into bed.'

Maya stood there, listening. The steps went on, down the lane, through the side gate, down the path, round into the back garden, on to the far end, through the other gate, round the next part of the building.

'It's Dad,' said Mum.

Maya turned and saw Mum already in bed, the duvet back.

'Come on,' said Mum. 'It's Dad's footsteps. Nobody else's.'

Maya darted into bed and bundled into Mum's arms.

'Poor love,' whispered Mum.

They held each other. Maya took a long breath, drank in the warmth of the bed, and Mum's body. Mum kissed her, stroked her head, started to sing.

'Did you not hear my lady, go down the garden singing?'

Maya closed her eyes.

'Remember it?' said Mum. 'When you were tiny?'

'You sang it,' said Maya. 'When I couldn't sleep.'

Mum gave her a squeeze and sang on.

'Blackbird and thrush were silent, to hear the alleys ringing.'

The footsteps came again, on the other side of the building.

'Oh, saw you not my lady, out in the garden there?'

Mum lowered her voice.

'Shaming the rose and lily, for she is twice as fair.'

Then a new voice, Dad's, under their window.

'Who's there?'

Maya sat sharply up, Mum with her. From below came a scrambling sound.

'Who's there?' said Dad again.

'Stay here,' said Mum, and she jumped out of bed.

'Mum—'

'Stay here. I'll close the door behind me. You'll be quite safe.'

And Mum was gone. Maya heard the thump of Mum's footsteps as she hurried along the corridor, down the stairs, out into the lane, round to the side of the hotel. Then nothing. No voices, no further steps, no sound of movement.

The Rowan Tree was silent too.

She climbed out of bed. She didn't want to. She wanted to pull the duvet right over her, even here in Mum and Dad's room, but it was no good. She had to see what was happening. She walked over to the nearest window and peered out.

No one to be seen from here. Just the lane below and that was empty. She walked over to the next window and stared out. Below was the path that led down the side of The Rowan Tree to the garden at the back. There was no one there either.

But in the pasture beyond . . .

She peered out, searching the bushes on the far side of the wall. It was hard to be sure but it looked as though two figures were moving there, low to the ground. Then suddenly she caught it: the thing she feared most. But it wasn't coming from beyond the window. It was coming from behind her. On the outside of the bedroom door.

Scratch, scratch, scratch.

She screamed again.

11

The sun trickled in through the windows of the conservatory. Maya sat slumped in the armchair, Mum standing on one side, Dad the other, Tom sitting on the stool close by. Doctor Wade pulled up a chair and leaned forward. Maya looked at her and wondered what the woman really thought beneath the polished friendliness.

'Your father says it was an animal,' said Doctor Wade.

'I know,' said Maya. 'He's told me.'

Doctor Wade glanced at Dad.

'You didn't see what kind of an animal it was?'

'No,' said Dad. 'I just caught a movement in a clump of bushes.'

'Where was this?'

'In the pasture just beyond our boundary wall.'

'The one with the long grass?'

'Yes. You can see the bushes from our bedroom window. Anyway, I thought it was a person hiding there at first. That's why I called out. I heard another movement but I couldn't see clearly in the darkness. Then Paula came out and joined me.'

'I didn't see anything,' said Mum. 'Just the bushes. So we went closer and then I heard a scuffling sound. I still didn't see anything but Phil thinks he caught sight of something darting off.'

'Definitely an animal,' said Dad.

'You're absolutely certain?' said Doctor Wade.

'What is this?' said Dad. 'An interrogation?'

'Of course not,' said Doctor Wade. 'I just want us to be able to reassure Maya that there was nothing sinister out there.'

'I've already reassured her,' Dad grumbled. 'So has her mum. We spent most of the night trying to reassure her. That's why we're so knackered now.'

He gave a heavy sigh. Maya stared through the door into the dining room. The tables were all laid ready but only three were taken. A boy and a girl she hadn't seen before were serving the breakfasts.

'Who are they?' she said dully.

'Jake and Roxy,' said Mum. 'We took them on yesterday. They seem quite pleasant. Both sixteen. We've taken on a third person too.'

A fierce-looking woman appeared at the other door of the dining room.

'That's her,' said Mum. 'She's called Milly.'

'She's nicer than she looks,' muttered Dad.

'You didn't tell me about them,' said Maya.

'You had enough on your mind,' said Mum.

Maya went on staring at the three figures.

'They turned up looking for a job,' Mum went on, 'while you and Tom were in the forest. They've worked here before so they should know the ropes. But we'll see how they get on. They're all from the village.'

'Oh,' said Maya.

'Is that a problem?' said Dad.

'Just that they'll know about me,' she said. 'The girl from The Rowan Tree who makes things up.'

She saw Jake look up from Table Five, catch her eye and look away again. Milly took a tray from Roxy and disappeared into the kitchen. Roxy turned her attention to Table Seven.

79

'That's silly,' said Mum. 'Nobody thinks that about you.'

'Tell me about the scratching, Maya,' said Doctor Wade.

'Mum and Dad must have told you what I said.'

'You tell me.'

Maya caught Jake's eye again.

'Please,' said Doctor Wade.

'I heard it on my bedroom door first.'

'The outside of the door?'

'Yes,' said Maya.'

'How long did it go on for?'

'I don't know. I just screamed and screamed.'

'We came running in,' said Mum.

Maya looked down, pictures from last night floating in her mind.

'Go on,' said Doctor Wade. 'I know this is difficult, but do your best. It might help me to understand things better.'

It won't, thought Maya, but she went on.

'Mum took me through to their bedroom.'

'Your mum and dad's room?'

'Yes. Dad went outside to check round. I cuddled up with Mum in bed. Then we heard Dad call out and ask if there was somebody there. Mum ran out—'

'Did she close the door after her?'

'Yes. And she went to help Dad.'

'OK,' said Doctor Wade. 'And while they were checking the bushes, you heard the scratching sound again?'

'Yes.'

'On the outside of your parents' door?'

'Yes.'

'Then what happened?'

'I screamed my head off,' said Maya. 'I just screamed and screamed. When I stopped, Mum and Dad were back in the room, and Tommy was there too, and lots of the guests were looking in, asking questions. And now some of them have checked out early.'

She looked at Dad.

'Haven't they?'

Dad didn't answer. He was staring into the dining room. Maya stared too and saw Milly, Jake, and Roxy gathered round the far door where a figure was trying push past them.

'Bonny,' she murmured.

As she spoke, the girl forced her way into the dining room, strode past the breakfast tables, and burst into the conservatory. She made straight for Dad.

'What's this about you sacking me?' she said.

'Bonny,' he began.

'I just spoke to Milly. She says you don't want me.'

Milly appeared, breathing hard.

'I'm terribly sorry, Mr Munro.'

'It's OK, Milly,' said Dad. 'I'll talk to Bonny.'

'I tried to—'

'Don't worry about it, Milly. Go back to work.'

Milly turned back to the dining room.

'Why am I sacked?' said Bonny.

Dad motioned her towards the door.

'Let's talk about this somewhere else.'

'No, let's talk about it here,' said Bonny.

Dad glowered but Bonny simply glared back. Maya saw the guests in the dining room watching.

'You haven't been sacked,' said Dad, 'because we never took you on. We gave you one shift. That's all. We never promised you any more work.'

'Are you saying I didn't do a good job?'

'You did an excellent job,' said Dad, 'and we're very grateful to you for it. But you did run off rather abruptly without giving us a chance to talk further.'

'I had to go,' said Bonny.

'Fair enough,' said Dad. 'But as you can see, we've now taken on new staff.'

'I'm better than them. Better than Jake and Roxy put together. And Milly.'

Bonny turned suddenly, as though she'd sensed something behind her. Maya stared past her and saw two police officers standing in the entrance to the dining room.

She recognized them at once: DI Henderson and DC Coker. To her relief, there was no sign of Annie Shaw. The two men spoke briefly to Milly, then walked across the dining room and into the conservatory.

'Good morning,' said DI Henderson, glancing round.

He fixed his eyes on Bonny. She folded her arms.

'Looking for me, big man?'

'Worked that out, did you?' he said.

'Lucky guess.'

DI Henderson smiled.

'Then you'll probably know what we want to talk to you about.'

'I'm not telling you where Mo is,' she said. 'I'm not telling anyone. He's freaked, OK? Scared out of his head. He was freaking bad enough already with the forest getting creepy and dead foxes turning up. But he's picked up something else too and it's spooking him even more.'

'What's spooking him?' said DI Henderson.

'Everything,' said Bonny, 'and everybody. Specially people who try and make him talk when they know he can't. And that includes you lot.'

'We haven't seen him,' said the officer. 'That's the point. That's why we're here. We heard about the business with the dead fox.'

'Who from?'

'Frank McMurdo. He and Bryn tried to catch Mo but he got away.'

'Too bad.'

'So we were hoping you might tell us where he is.' DI Henderson frowned. 'But you can be hard to find too.'

'Your problem, not mine,' said Bonny.

'No doubt,' said the officer. 'But now that we have found you, I'd be grateful for a little talk.'

'Bit busy right now.'

'It's for Mo's sake as much as anything else.'

'Yeah, right,' said Bonny. 'Like I believe that.'

'Come on, Bonny,' said DC Coker. 'What did he do with the fox?'

'Don't know.'

'Where is he?'

'Got to go.'

DI Henderson blocked the way.

'You arresting me?' said Bonny.

'No, I'm simply—'

'Then I'm off.'

Bonny made for the door. DC Coker stepped in front of her. She snarled up at him.

'You arresting me, yes or no?'

DC Coker glanced at his colleague, then back at Bonny.

'We're not arresting you.'

'Then piss off!' said Bonny. She turned to Dad. 'And you and your family can piss off too!'

And she slipped through the door into the dining room. She stopped at the first table where Mr and Mrs Jacobs were finishing breakfast, bent down and in one movement, swept the cups, plates, and teapot off the table and sent them smashing on the floor.

'Come back here!' roared Dad and he made to run after her.

DI Henderson caught him by the arm.

'Leave it, sir. We'll deal with it.'

The two officers hurried out of the conservatory. Bonny had already disappeared but Maya could hear her screaming as she smashed the vases in the hall and the plant pots outside The Rowan Tree, before running off down the lane.

'Bloody hell,' said Tom.

Dad looked round at them.

'I'd better get busy.'

Milly appeared in the doorway. Behind her in the dining room Jake and Roxy were sweeping up the broken crockery from the floor. The guests had all gone.

'I'm coming,' said Dad.

'Mr and Mrs Jacobs is checking out,' said Milly. 'Think others is too.'

'No surprise.' Dad turned back to Maya. 'Listen, sweetheart. We're going to have to talk later about last night, OK? Just take it easy for a bit and stick with Tom. I don't know what it is about The Rowan Tree that's upsetting you but we'll get to the bottom of it.'

'Mr Munro?' said Milly.

Dad looked round at her.

'If you want to know about The Rowan Tree,' she said, 'then Jake's the person to talk to. His family used to own this place. Long time back. And he's worked here since he was a kid. Every holiday to earn money. So he knows The Rowan Tree better than anyone.'

'I'll bear that in mind,' said Dad. 'But right now he's got work to do. And Maya needs to speak to Doctor Wade.'

He gave Maya a kiss.

'Everything's going to be fine. And don't worry about Bonny. She's just hot air.'

And he set off with Milly. Maya leaned back in the

armchair, suddenly very tired. She saw Doctor Wade watching her closely.

'Doctor Wade?' she said.

'Yes, Maya?'

'I'm not ill.'

'I know you're not,' said Doctor Wade. 'You're scared.'

'Have you got any pills for scared?'

'I'm not sure pills are what you need right now. But I do have one suggestion. I suggest you take that woman's advice. About the young man who knows about this place. What was his name?'

'Jake,' said Mum.

'Right,' said Doctor Wade. 'Why not get Jake to take Maya round The Rowan Tree and tell her about it?'

'But Maya already knows The Rowan Tree,' said Mum. 'We all do.'

'I doubt that very much,' said Doctor Wade. 'An old hotel like this. How long have you been here?'

'Well, just a few days,' said Mum, 'but do you think we didn't look the place over thoroughly when we bought it?'

'I'm sure you did,' said Doctor Wade. 'But this boy grew up here. He'll know every nook and cranny. He'll also know any rumours in the village about The Rowan Tree. It's just a thought. Maya's frightened of the place and Jake just might be able to answer her questions and put her mind at rest.'

'Or do the opposite,' said Tom.

'What do you mean?' said Mum.

'He might scare her even more. If he tells her something really creepy.'

Maya looked at him.

'Tommy?'

'Yeah?'

'I want to know more about The Rowan Tree.'

'OK,' said Tom. 'But I'm coming with you. You're not going round with Jake on your own. And listen . . . '

Tom leaned closer.

'If he starts doing your head in, I'll have him.'

12

The tour of The Rowan Tree was soon over. It was obvious to Maya that Jake had no idea what he was really being asked to do, that Tom's only concern was to make sure this new boy didn't get too close to his sister; and for her part, she felt too embarrassed to bring up the questions she really wanted to ask.

'Want to see up there?' said Jake.

They were standing at the bottom of the steps leading to the attic room.

'That used to be my old room,' he said. 'So I'm told.'

'So I'm told?' said Tom. 'What does that mean?'

Jake kept his eyes on Maya.

'It's got a secret compartment,' he said.

She had no interest in going up. She'd seen the attic room and there was nothing in it but junk they'd brought from London and hadn't had time to sort. She stared back at Jake, wondering what he thought of her.

'So what's this all about?' he said suddenly.

She bit her lip, unsure whether to trust him.

'Go on,' he said.

'Are they talking about me in the village?' she asked.

'Quite a bit.'

'Do they think I'm a fantasist?'

'I don't really care what they think,' said Jake. 'Are you a fantasist?'

'No.'

'That's OK, then.'

He glanced up the stairs.

'So you don't want to see the attic room?'

'You never answered my question,' said Tom.

Jake sat down on the stairs and looked at him.

'I've forgotten what it was.'

'No, you haven't,' said Tom.

The two boys stared at each other.

'Try me again,' said Jake.

'You said it used to be your old room,' said Tom, 'and then you said, "So I'm told". That doesn't make sense. You either remember your room or you don't.'

'Not if you only slept in it as a baby,' said Jake.

Tom said nothing.

'I was born in The Rowan Tree,' said Jake. 'My mum and dad used to own the place. But they split up. I don't remember any of it. Or them. My mum walked out when I was two. My dad died a few weeks later.'

'I'm sorry,' said Maya.

'You don't need to be,' said Jake. 'I never knew them so I don't miss them. I'm fine about it. But anyway, the attic room up there . . .'

He nodded towards it.

'That's where my parents slept. And I was in a cot in the same room.' He glanced at Tom. 'So I'm told.'

'How did your dad die?' said Tom.

'Tommy,' said Maya, 'you shouldn't ask—'

'It's OK,' said Jake. 'Ask anything you want. He fell over outside The Rose and Crown. He'd had too much to drink. Hit his head on that big stone water trough and lost consciousness. Never came back. So Uncle Frank said.'

'Uncle Frank?'

'Frank McMurdo, the forester. You've met him. He told me.'

'Yeah, we met him,' said Tom. 'He was really rude.'

'He's like that with everybody,' said Jake. 'Don't let it get to you. He's OK underneath. I live with him, so I know what I'm talking about.'

'You live with him?' said Tom.

'Yep.'

'I can't believe he's your uncle,' said Maya.

'Well, he is,' said Jake. 'My dad was his little brother.'

'So you're a McMurdo too?'

'Yeah. And with my dad dead and my mum God knows where, I've lived with Uncle Frank since I was two. He's been good to me, better than my father probably. He says my dad was a bit of a nightmare, specially when he was drunk.'

'Was that why your mum walked out?' said Tom.

'Tommy,' said Maya.

'It's OK,' said Jake. 'I just said. Ask me anything you want.'

'So was it?' said Tom.

'Could have been,' said Jake. 'But it might have been her too. Uncle Frank says most people didn't like her. I don't think about her much.'

'Why not?' said Tom.

'Because she never thought about me,' said Jake. 'Never came back after my dad died, never bothered checking if I was all right. So I'm not much interested in her. She could be dead too for all I know. Anyway . . . '

He looked at Maya.

'What's this all about? You still haven't told me.'

'I'm scared of The Rowan Tree,' she said.

'Why?'

'There's something wrong here.'

She studied his face, terrified that he was going to laugh at her.

89

'Does that sound stupid?' she said.

'No.'

Jake leaned back on the stairs, still watching her.

'I don't know about something being wrong here,' he said, 'but I'll tell you one thing about The Rowan Tree. It's never seemed a happy place. Not to me anyway. My parents weren't happy here. And the people who took over after them weren't happy either.'

'How many owners have there been?' said Tom.

'Just Mr and Mrs Flint.'

'Flint?' said Maya.

'Yeah.'

'I met someone yesterday called Rebecca Flint.'

'That's Mrs Flint.'

'She said she never wanted to come inside The Rowan Tree again.'

'Well, she's probably still bitter,' said Jake. 'Her husband went off with another woman just before Christmas. Don't know where. And The Rowan Tree went on the market in January. Mrs Flint's stayed on in Hembury.'

'Where does she live?'

'Outskirts of the village. She's got a place with a bit of land. Keeps hens and stuff. Most people think she's a bit of a snob, but I like her. She was fine with me when I worked here. Mr Flint was a lazy bastard. But you must know about the Flints. You bought The Rowan Tree from them.'

Tom shook his head.

'Mum and Dad bought The Rowan Tree through an agent and it was all done in a rush. They only closed the deal a few weeks ago. If the Flints moved out at Christmas, that's probably why we never heard about them.'

Jake stood up.

'Sure you don't want to see my old room?'

'Did you say it's got a secret compartment?' said Tom.

'Yeah, but it's pretty boring,' said Jake. 'Come on. I'll show you anyway.'

They climbed the stairs and entered the attic room.

'I won't give you any clues,' said Jake.

Maya said nothing. She could feel something she didn't like; something she'd sensed before. She glanced around her at the boxes and tea chests.

'See if you can find it without my help,' said Jake.

Tom started tapping walls.

'Could be any of these,' he said.

Maya walked over to the window and looked out. The lane stretched away towards the village square. She stared down it, past the houses, past The Rose and Crown, past the church, and on to where the forest started.

Tom's voice came from behind her.

'It's got to be in here.'

She went on staring out. She could see figures walking about the square, McMurdo and Bryn coming out of the pub, carrying mugs of beer. She turned and saw Tom bent over, feeling round the skirting board.

Jake was watching her.

'Call me a genius,' said Tom.

She and Jake both looked at him. He caught their eyes and pointed to where the panelling opened out. Inside was a small compartment with nothing in it but dust.

'Told you it was boring,' said Jake. 'You could hide a cat in there but not much else. There's another secret compartment in the broom cupboard on the first floor. But it's not much better.'

Tom started to push the panelling back.

'Maya?' said Jake.

She looked at him.

'Something's scaring you,' he said.

Tom straightened up.

'Sis? You all right?'

'Is it in this room?' said Jake.

The two boys stood there, looking at her.

'Can you stop doing that?' she said.

'Doing what?' said Tom.

'Staring at me.' She half-turned away. 'Listen, I just need to be by myself for a bit.'

'I'm supposed to be keeping an eye on you,' said Tom.

'I'll be fine.'

'Mum said I had to stick close to you. And make sure you don't go outside The Rowan Tree.'

'I won't.'

'She'll kill me if you do. She said so.'

'I won't. I promise.'

Maya set off down the stairs. Tom ran after her and caught her at the bottom.

'Maybe have a rest,' he said.

'I'm fine, Tommy.'

'You didn't sleep much last night. Have a rest in your room.'

'OK, I'll do that. Thanks, Tommy.'

She set off down the corridor.

A rest in her room.

She frowned. She hadn't been in there since she left it last night. She walked up to the door, stared at it for a few moments, then turned away; and there it was again: that feeling of something dangerous and familiar.

And close.

She walked back down the corridor. All was quiet in The Rowan Tree, especially now that the guests had gone, but from the attic room above came the sound of Tom and Jake laughing. She moved on down the corridor.

The feeling was still there and it was stronger towards

the back of the hotel. She stopped outside Room Seven, listening hard. No further laughter from the attic room, nor any other voices. She pushed open the door, stepped in and closed it behind her, then walked over to the window.

Nothing suspicious in the garden: just the lawn, the path, the empty tables. She heard the door open behind her. She whirled round and saw Milly standing there.

'Oh, Maya,' she said. 'I didn't know you was in here.'

'I was just . . . '

'I've come to make the bed.'

'Sorry.'

'No need to say sorry,' said Milly. 'You live here, remember?'

'I know but—'

'Stay if you want.' Milly smiled. 'I wouldn't mind some company.'

'No, it's OK,' said Maya. 'I'll just . . . '

She stared out of the window again, and there it was, out in the garden, just below the window: the fox looking up at her.

Milly spoke from the doorway.

'What are you looking at, love?'

The fox turned and darted off towards the back door. It lingered there for a moment, looking back, then disappeared round the side of the building. Maya peered after it, knowing it was waiting. She turned towards the door.

'Everything all right, Maya?' said Milly.

'Fine,' she said.

And she hurried out of the room and down the stairs.

13

The fox was nowhere to be seen. She stood outside the back door and stared into the garden. All was still. The flowers, the bushes, the trees. The sun blazed upon an unmoving space. She walked to the side of the hotel and checked down the path, the way she'd seen the animal go.

It wasn't there now. She turned back to the garden and scanned the lawn. She could sense the fox watching her, as aware of her as she was of it, more so; and there was something else, something even more disturbing.

'Why am I following it?' she murmured.

She knew she shouldn't be. It was insane, just like the first time when she'd run off into the forest and found the bodies. She'd seen the fox on the path and without a word to Tom, she'd followed it; and now here she was, doing the same thing again.

'I won't follow you this time,' she muttered.

Then she saw it.

Beyond the top table, close to the shrubbery.

Digging in the ground with its paws.

She watched. The animal didn't look up but went on scrabbling in the ground. She started to walk towards it. Some part of her protested but she ignored it and carried on. She wouldn't go close, she told herself. She'd stay in control, just scare it off.

She reached the top table.

The fox froze, its yellow eyes drilling her. She stopped too and stared back. The animal studied her for what seemed a long time, then started scrabbling in the ground again.

'What are you digging for?' she said.

She could see nothing unusual, just roots and twigs. The fox looked up again, fixed her with its eyes, then shook itself, turned and loped towards the gate; then stopped again.

She frowned. It hadn't run out into the pasture beyond, yet it could easily have done so. The gate was half-open and the long grass was just a short distance away. But the fox was still here, its eyes drilling her as before.

'I'm not coming with you this time,' she said.

The animal crouched low, still watching her.

'I told you,' she said. 'I'm not coming.'

Again the fox started to scrabble in the ground. No roots to pick at this time, just the grass that bordered the path to the gate, and nothing worth digging for as far as she could see. She walked forward again, in spite of her fear. The fox didn't move but went on picking at the grass.

'I wouldn't do that, Foxy,' she said. 'You'll have my dad after you.'

They were close now, too close. She stopped—and the fox moved at once, down the path, through the gate, into the pasture. But still it wouldn't bolt. She could see it through the gap, watching her from the edge of the long grass.

'I'm not bloody coming,' she said.

But her feet were moving. She stared down at them in horror.

'Stop,' she told them.

They carried on walking.

'Stop!'

The feet stopped. She stood there, daring them to move. They stayed still, but only just. She could feel every part of her straining towards the fox. She looked up again. The animal was still there, digging in the ground, but suddenly it fixed her with its eyes, shot off to the right and disappeared behind the wall that bordered the garden. She ran to the gate, pulled it fully open and stared round.

Nothing.

The sun vanished behind a cloud.

'Where are you?' she said. 'You're still close. I know you are. You haven't gone.'

She ran her eye over the pasture. Nothing moved in the long grass, not even the grass itself.

'You're close,' she said. 'You're really close.'

Then she caught it, over by the clump of bushes below Mum and Dad's bedroom window; where Dad had seen something last night. The fox was digging as before, and now there was something frantic about it. Earth and twigs were flying. Then once again, the animal stopped and stared straight at her.

'No,' she muttered.

She felt her feet stir.

'No.'

Her right foot moved, her left, her right.

'No!' she snarled.

They came to a halt.

'Maya?' said a voice.

She turned and saw Roxy standing by the open gate.

'Who are you talking to?' said the girl.

Maya glanced back at the bushes. As she'd expected, the fox was gone. So was the pressure in her feet. She took a slow breath, walked back into the garden and closed the gate behind her.

'Your mum and dad sent me to find you,' said Roxy.

'They're worried about me,' said Maya.

She leaned back against the gate.

'I've scared all the guests away, haven't I?'

'Bonny helped you,' said Roxy.

Maya shook her head.

'I freaked them out before Bonny turned up. It's my fault they've gone.'

She stared over the garden. It seemed empty of life. No insects buzzed, no bees hummed, no birds clung to the feeders.

'Roxy?'

'Yeah?'

'Do you think I'm off my head?'

'Maybe a bit.'

They glanced at each other.

'Maybe a lot,' said Maya.

They smiled, looked away.

'I don't really think that,' said Roxy. 'Neither does Jake.'

'How do you know?'

'He told me.'

'You good mates?'

'Yeah.' Roxy paused. 'Nothing more.'

Maya tensed. She could feel the movement in her feet again. With an effort she stepped away from the gate, then turned to face it. She knew the fox was on the other side, its eyes peering towards her.

'Why me?' she whispered.

'You're doing it again,' said Roxy. 'Talking to nobody.'

She went on staring at the gate. The fox was still there. She could feel it pulling her towards it. She reached out to open the gate. As she did so, she felt the strain ease and she knew that the fox had run away again.

But it hadn't gone far. It was somewhere over to the right. She could sense it prowling there. She glanced along the garden wall, picturing the pasture beyond and the bushes where she'd last seen the animal. She was certain it had returned there.

But why? And what did it want from her?

'You're starting to scare me,' said Roxy.

'I'm sorry,' said Maya.

She looked back at the girl and forced another smile.

'Who were you talking to?' said Roxy.

'It doesn't matter.'

She saw Mum and Dad walking up the garden path towards them.

'Everything OK?' said Dad.

Mum stepped quickly forward.

'It's not,' she said. 'I can see.'

She took Maya by the hand.

'What's happened?'

'Nothing.'

'Roxy?'

'Nothing's happened,' said Maya. 'Roxy found me here. That's all.'

'You didn't go outside, did you?' said Dad.

'Not really.'

'What does that mean?'

'I was just standing by the gate looking out.'

Mum glanced at Roxy.

'Thanks for finding Maya. That's really good of you. Now go and get a bite to eat. There's some food laid out in the kitchen. I think Tom and Jake have already started so you'd better get in quick.'

Roxy turned and left. Mum looked at Maya again.

'Now what's up?'

'Nothing, Mum.'

'So why do you keep looking at that wall?'

'I didn't know I was.'

'You're doing it all the time,' said Dad.

Mum led her over to the nearest table.

'Let's sit down,' she said.

They pulled the chairs close and sat down.

'You're not in trouble with us,' said Mum. 'It's just that you keep looking at that wall, like you're really frightened of it. So I'm wondering what's wrong.'

Maya glanced back at it; and there was the presence of the fox again.

Peering at her from the other side.

'I can't explain it,' she said.

'And you don't have to,' said Dad. 'Not if you don't want to. Or if you can't. Just promise us you won't go outside The Rowan Tree.'

'Just for the moment,' said Mum. 'While you get yourself straight.'

'OK,' said Maya.

The fox went on watching her from beyond the wall. She could picture it so clearly it was as though she was looking straight at it.

'Sweetheart?' said Mum. 'Can you look back at us now?'

Maya turned to face them again.

'Mum?' she said.

'Yes, darling.'

'Can I sleep with you again tonight?'

'Of course you can,' said Mum.

Milly appeared with a plate of sandwiches.

'Thought I'd better rescue these for you,' she said, 'before the boys finished everything.'

'Thanks, Milly,' said Dad.

Milly put the plate down on the table.

'Tuck into some of these, Maya. Go on.'

'All quiet, Milly?' said Dad.

'Yes, Mr Munro.'

Dad grunted.

'You'd think somebody might want a room,' he said. 'Or a meal in the restaurant. Or a drink. Or a coffee.'

'Oh, we did have a restaurant booking,' said Milly. 'I forgot to tell you. Tomorrow evening at seven. Table for two. He came in an hour ago and fixed it.'

'Who?'

'Bryn Fossett.'

Maya sat up. Milly looked at her.

'Remember him, Maya? Assistant forester? Guy with red hair?'

'I remember.'

'Who's his dinner guest?' said Dad.

'He didn't say,' said Milly. 'But everyone in Hembury'll know the answer.'

Maya turned back in the direction of the pasture.

'Annie Shaw,' she murmured.

And something growled beyond the wall.

14

She lay in the big double-bed, Mum fast asleep beside her, and let her eyes wander yet again to the clock. Quarter past midnight and she was still wide awake. But she'd known it would be like this. She twisted onto her back and stared up at the ceiling.

Silence, apart from Mum's breathing and her own, but her attention was on neither. It was on the sound she was listening for. Yet so far there had been no scratching on the door. Just a moan as Mum rolled the other way.

Then a growl outside the window.

She sat up and stared towards it. She knew the fox was still out there. It had never left the pasture. She'd sensed its presence all through the afternoon and into the night, though she'd stayed inside The Rowan Tree and refused to look out.

Another growl.

She climbed out of bed, crept to the window and eased back the edge of the curtain. There was the path round the side of the building, and the wall, and beyond that the pasture outside The Rowan Tree. She ran her eyes over the long grass and then the bushes near the top.

The fox was easy to see.

It wanted to be seen.

And to see her.

She shuddered. There was no mistaking this. The animal was in exactly the same place as before, by the

101

bushes just down from the window, and its yellow eyes were peering straight up at her. The moment it saw her, it started to scrabble in the ground again with its paws.

She watched, nervously. This didn't make sense. The fox couldn't—it simply couldn't—be trying to communicate with her. It stopped digging suddenly and stared up at her again. Its eyes seemed to blaze at her. She let go of the curtain, unable to look, and stood there, breathing hard.

One minute, two minutes, five, ten.

She pulled the curtain aside again.

And there were the eyes, watching her as before, as though they'd never left the window and had simply been waiting for her to reappear; and now that she was back again, the animal began scrabbling once more in the grassy ground. She let the curtain fall and turned to the bed, fear running through her.

And the ghost of an idea.

She knew it was stupid. She knew she shouldn't even think about it, especially after what Mum and Dad had said to her about not going outside. But there was nothing else for it. She had to find out what the fox was digging for. It was clear that the creature was never going to leave her in peace. Whatever this was about, it involved her.

She looked at Mum, still fast asleep.

'Sorry,' she mouthed.

She pulled on her clothes and stole out of the room. All was still in the corridor. She could hear the sound of Mum's breathing back in the main bedroom, but that was all. She tiptoed down to Tom's door. Steady breathing there too. She moved on to Room Three and listened again.

Nothing.

But the door was ajar. She inched it open and peered round. Dad was curled up in bed, one arm twisted over his head, but he too was asleep. She made her way down the stairs and through the silent corridors to the back door.

Again the doubts came rushing in. She quelled them and picked up the torch. She had to sort this thing—but she'd make it quick: just check out the bushes and come straight back. She opened the door as quietly as she could and slipped out.

The garden looked eerie in the night, the moon-glow catching the water in the bird bath, shadows clipping the tables and chairs. But she could see her way clearly. She kept the torch switched off, cut across to the shed, pulled out the nearest spade, and hurried to the gate.

Still silence. She stood there for a few seconds, listening hard. Nothing at first, then . . . she was sure she caught it: the soft scatter of earth over to the right. She crept out into the pasture.

She was breathing faster now, shivering too, though the night was warm. It wasn't just the presence of the fox over by the bushes; it was this new, unfamiliar ground. She and Tom had had no time to explore the land on this side of The Rowan Tree and the grass was much taller than it had seemed from the gate.

But she could still make out the bushes over to the right.

And hear the scrabbling paws.

She started in that direction, clasping the spade tight. No sign of the fox yet, just the bushes and what appeared to be small mounds of earth in the lower ground to the left. She walked on warily, peering ahead.

Closer, closer, just a few feet now from the bushes. She could see the fox at last. It was down in a small crater which it appeared to have dug by itself. She could see more mounds of earth thrown up around it, and the animal was digging furiously into the base.

She stopped, just back from the edge, and watched. The fox turned its head, took her in with its eyes, then carried on digging. But there was no clue as to what it was looking for. All she could see was earth and more earth. She took another step closer. The fox went on digging, its paws worrying at the soil.

She hesitated, stepped closer still. She was in touching distance of the animal now. It seemed not to care. She stared down at the ground where its paws were moving, but as before there was nothing to see but earth.

She glanced up towards the bushes at the top of the crater, then beyond them to The Rowan Tree. No lights were on, no curtains drawn back; no sign of life. Except down here.

She looked at the fox again.

And as she did so, it turned towards her and snarled.

She jumped back, clutching the spade in front of her. The animal was watching her fiercely, its eyes brighter than before. She realized she'd come much too close. It snarled again.

'Don't hurt me,' she said.

As if in answer, the fox leapt out of the crater, tore away to the left and disappeared in the long grass. She stared after it, trembling, but there was no further sign of it. She turned back to the base of the crater where the fox had been digging.

All was dark here, even with the moonlight slanting down. She switched on the torch and shone the beam in, but she could see nothing to explain the digging, nothing to justify creeping out here in the middle of the night. She stepped down into the crater, flicked the beam of the torch about.

Still no clue as to what the fox had been looking for. Maybe this was all quite normal, just an animal foraging for food. She knew nothing about the habits of foxes. Perhaps they did this kind of thing. She flicked the beam again—and something glinted in the light.

Something yellow; something dead.

She edged back. No more searching was needed now. It was obvious what this was and there was nothing to be gained by staying out here. The animal had been seeking one of its own and she had no wish to dig up the corpse of another fox.

Then the yellow thing moved.

She gave a start.

But all was still again, save for a thin stream of soil falling from the top of the nearest mound. She had to get out of here, run back to The Rowan Tree. She turned to go, but as she did so, the beam of the torch caught something else.

She stopped, trying to pretend she hadn't seen it.

But it was no good. The fox was not the only thing buried here. She swallowed hard, bent down, saw the dead eyes staring up at her, and then the other thing. She reached out with the tip of the spade.

Nothing moved at first, but she was barely touching the soil. She forced herself to probe round the outside of the fox's face, ease out the loose earth. Suddenly it fell away.

There was the fox's head—and no body to go with it. It rolled down in front of her, staring blankly up. But she barely saw it. Her eyes were fixed on what had been underneath.

A human foot.

'Oh, Christ,' she murmured.

It was protruding from the broken soil: a bare sole, grimy and scratched, the toes close together, the rest of the body hidden from view. She scrambled out of the crater. She had to get back, raise the alarm.

She threw a glance up at The Rowan Tree. Still no lights on. She pictured Mum's sleeping figure, just a short distance away. Maybe even in shouting distance. Then something blocked her view. Something dark, rising from the bushes.

A figure with a fox's face.

15

And it wasn't just the face. The figure was human but the body too was swathed in fox-fur. Arms, legs, torso—all were covered. How many foxes had died to create such a disguise she could not guess, but it hardly mattered.

What mattered was running.

She dropped the torch and spade and tore for the gate. But it was no good. The figure quickly outpaced her, keeping left to cut her off from The Rowan Tree, then moving close. She blundered right, tramping over the edge of the pasture. The figure stayed with her, blocking any way back.

She heard a hissing sound behind her shoulder.

She threw a glance round and saw the fox-face leering. Another hiss, then a laugh from beneath the mask. She started to scream. It was a puny sound, swallowed by her breaths, and it died on the night air.

Another laugh, closer still.

She lurched to the right again, crashing into the long grass. She had no idea where she was going. Some part of her tried to think. She hadn't been caught and she didn't know why. The figure was faster and stronger than she was. She threw another glance over her shoulder.

And saw no one.

She stopped and looked back. All she could see was the long grass, the bushes where she'd been digging, the sanctuary of The Rowan Tree beyond. It stood there, bathed in moonlight, just a short sprint away if she could get there. Then the fox-figure rose from the long grass.

Blocking her way again.

'What do you want?' she called.

The figure ran towards her. She turned and raced on across the pasture, her eyes searching for a way out. To the right was the lane that led back to the village, but she could see at once that the wall was too high to climb, and there was no sign of a gate.

Straight ahead, another wall, also too high; to the left, small trees and a third stone wall, but there was a stile at the end. She heard harsh, exaggerated breaths close behind her and put on speed.

The laugh came again. It seemed to wrap round her. She looked back and saw that the figure had vanished once more. She stopped, gasping for air, and searched the long grass. Another laugh. She stared round, trying to work out which direction it had come from.

More laughs, one after the other, broken by periods of silence, each laugh seeming to come from a different spot. She was turning desperately now, trying to see the figure and know which way to run.

Yet another laugh, somewhere to the left, it seemed, from the direction of The Rowan Tree. She ran the other way, towards the stile at the end of the wall. The figure appeared at once in the long grass.

Directly in front of her.

She drew up and screamed.

'Go away!'

The figure rushed forward, growling. She stepped to the side and somehow slipped past, but it had been too easy, and now she knew why. This was a game and she was sport. She reached the stile and scrambled over it into the meadow beyond. The fox-figure leapt after her.

She stumbled on, all direction lost, plunging through paddocks and pastures and rough-ploughed fields. Somewhere near she sensed the forest, breathing in the night, but nearer still was the fox-figure, taunting her from hidden places.

She knew she couldn't escape. She was too easy to catch. She'd be taken when it was time for the kill. She staggered into a new field and saw a barn in front of her. She drew up, panting, unable to run any more.

She'd lost all sense of where she was, or where the figure was. Watching her now, that was for sure. She hobbled up to the entrance of the barn and stopped outside it. She knew she had nothing left. She glanced round at the building. A derelict shell, roof stove in.

A lonely place to die.

She caught the sound of a step. She didn't move. She knew there was no point. More steps, moving slowly, then the familiar laugh; and there was the figure, just a few feet away. The eyes inside the fox-mask glowed. She heard a mocking voice, a voice she knew.

'Going to give me a good time, townie?'

So it was Zep. She'd suspected it. He was grinning at her, chuckling and gloating over his prize. She thought of the body buried under the bushes outside The Rowan Tree. Maybe Zep would bury her there too. When he'd had his fun.

She felt a chill pass through her.

'Leave me alone, Zep,' she said.

'I don't think so.'

She sensed the change in him. The mockery was gone, the laughter, the leering. He moved towards her, his body quivering.

'Zep, don't.'

'Come on, townie. Why waste an opportunity?'

'Leave me alone.'

He pushed himself up against her.

'I know what you want,' he muttered.

'I want you to go away.'

'No, you don't.'

She squirmed back from him. He reached out, caught hold of her shoulder. She screamed. He forced himself up against her again—then, to her surprise, let go. She took a step back and stared at him.

He wasn't moving. He was just standing there in front of her. She peered at the eyes in the slits of the fox-mask. They were fixed, but not on her. They were staring past her shoulder at something behind her.

She didn't turn to look. She went on watching Zep's eyes. Whatever was behind her, he was the greater danger. He went on staring past her, then slowly took a step back, and then another, and another.

She watched, trembling, but he went on backing away, slowly, slowly, watching her again now; then suddenly he turned, vaulted the stile at the bottom of the field and disappeared in the night. Maya spun round and saw a huge form in the entrance to the barn.

'Mo,' she said.

The boy stood there, watching her.

'Thank you,' she said. 'Thank you so much.'

Mo looked down at his watch. She saw his lips silently moving.

'You're waiting for Bonny,' she said. 'You're counting the seconds.'

Mo went on studying his watch.

'She's given you a time, hasn't she?' said Maya. 'She's told you to wait here till a certain time and then . . .'

But it was no good. She couldn't think any more, couldn't speak. She burst into tears. She didn't try to hold them back. She just slumped to the ground, plunged her face into her hands, and howled.

It was some time before she stopped, and even when she did, she kept her hands over her face. She didn't know whether Mo was still standing there. She'd lost all awareness of him while she was crying.

He'd probably walked off. He certainly hadn't tried to comfort her in any way, or make contact with her. She took her hands from her face and looked up. The boy was still standing there, on exactly the same spot, counting the seconds on his watch.

She was desperate to get home now but it was hard to know what to do. Mo was a whole new problem. He'd saved her from Zep but she couldn't get involved in whatever he was doing out here. She had a buried body to report, and an attempted rape at the very least. Yet getting home wouldn't be easy.

She made herself stand up.

'Thank you again,' she said. 'I don't know what would have happened if you hadn't been here.'

Mo went on studying his watch; then suddenly he looked up at her. She stared back at him and saw the dark intensity she'd noticed before in his strange, disturbing eyes. She couldn't begin to imagine what he was thinking.

She glanced round at the stile. She had no idea how to get home and the thought of trying to find her way back alone terrified her. Zep was still at large and quite possibly watching them right this moment and waiting for another chance.

But there was one possibility.

A remote one.

'Mo, will you walk back with me to The Rowan Tree?'

The boy showed no sign of having understood her. He stared at her for a while, then looked sharply down at his

111

watch again, his lips counting silently as before; and she knew he wouldn't move, not for her, not for anyone.

Even if he had understood her, he wouldn't move till Bonny arrived and told him what to do next. She looked back at the stile, tried to work out which way to go—but in her heart she knew she couldn't face it.

She would have to wait for Bonny too. However long it took.

Then Bonny's voice rang out.

'What the bloody hell are you doing here?'

16

The girl was standing behind them, at the far end of the barn, and appeared to have come upon them from the other side of the field. She was carrying a small rucksack. Maya looked at Mo and saw his body rigid, his eyes fixed on Bonny. The girl strode towards them.

'Bonny,' said Maya.

'Not now.'

Bonny stopped in front of Mo. 'Hey, big guy.'

'Bonny,' said Maya.

'I said not now.'

'Please help me.'

Bonny didn't answer. She just unshouldered the rucksack and handed it to Mo. He looked at her vacantly.

'Go on.' She pushed it at him. 'Take it and get started. I got your favourite.'

Mo took the rucksack.

'Start with the pie,' said Bonny. 'Eat the pie first. Eat all of it. Then drink some water. Drink half the bottle.'

Mo dipped a huge hand into the rucksack and pulled out a paper bag.

'Not that one,' said Bonny. 'That's the apple pie. That's for after. Find the pie in the silver foil.'

Mo pulled it out.

'Good boy,' said Bonny. 'Now put the apple pie back. That's it. Now eat the other pie. It's your favourite. Eat all of it. Take off the foil first.'

Mo did as he was told.

'Well done,' said Bonny.

'Bonny.' Maya took a step closer. 'I've been attacked. Zep chased me over the fields. He was wearing this . . . fox-fur disguise. He looked terrifying. He was going to rape me, maybe kill me. I got lost and ended up here and Mo . . . '

She looked round at the boy, now methodically eating.

'Mo saved me,' she said. 'He was great. But . . . '

She looked back at Bonny. The girl was watching her without much apparent interest.

'Bonny, listen, I found a body buried in the pasture outside The Rowan Tree.'

'A body?'

'Yes.'

'What kind of a body?'

'I don't know. I only saw the foot. But I've got to get back and report it.'

'Why didn't you report it before?'

'Because Zep suddenly turned up. Or he might have been there all along. He might even have buried the body. And killed whoever it was. I don't know. He chased me here and . . . '

She took some jerky breaths.

'Bonny, I've got to get back. But I'm scared. I don't know the way home and I don't know where Zep's gone. Please, Bonny, please help me get back. Or ring my mum and dad and tell them where we are so they can—'

'I haven't got a phone,' said Bonny.

Maya stared back, sensing the lie. But there was no point in challenging it. Bonny stood there, watching.

'Please get me back, Bonny,' said Maya.

She was close to tears again but determined not to break down. She felt sure Bonny would see tears as a ploy and refuse to help. She didn't suppose Bonny ever cried about anything. But the girl was clearly hesitating. Perhaps it was the business over losing her job at The Rowan Tree.

Mo gave a burp. Maya looked round at him. He'd finished the pie and was fiddling with the bottle of water. He saw Maya watching him and froze, as though unsettled by her gaze. She gave him a smile, the best she could manage.

'OK,' said Bonny.

Maya turned back to her.

'We'll take you home,' said the girl, 'but I need something in return.'

'I can't get you your job back,' said Maya. 'Dad won't listen to anything I say.'

'I'm not asking for my job back. I don't want it any more.'

'What do you want?'

'Silence,' said Bonny. 'From you. That's what I want. No telling anyone about me and Mo being here. It's a place we come, OK? A place where no one else comes much. We've got other places to go, places where we can sleep safe, but . . . '

Bonny glanced at Mo, then lowered her voice.

'Mo gets lost easy, right? He's not good at finding his way round. Mostly I have to show him where we're going. But this old barn . . . he can usually find his way here on his own. Don't ask me why. So I usually get him to wait for me here. If I've got to leave him for some reason.'

She glanced at the boy again, then back at Maya.

'So you keep quiet about seeing us here. We'll take you back to The Rowan Tree, but you haven't seen us, right? If anyone asks.'

'You mean the police?'

'I mean anyone,' said Bonny. 'Not just the police. We've got enemies, OK? Or Mo has. There's big trouble for him round Hembury. No one's ever understood him. Even people who act kind to him. None of 'em understand him, not like I do. I'm the only person he ever talks to, and he doesn't say much to me. Just mumbles a few words, and they don't always make a lot of sense. But I get him, most of the time. And I'm telling you . . . '

Bonny leaned closer.

'There's bad stuff going on round here, and now you're telling me about a dead body. That makes it worse. I'm even more worried about Mo. He's freaked out of his head already. He's no danger to anyone, and he can't talk anyway so he's never going to give anything away, but I think he knows who's behind all these things, and that person knows he knows, and they're after him.'

'Do you know who it is?'

'No,' said Bonny, 'but Mo's definitely picked something up. He likes the forest, or he used to. He feels safer with trees round him. Prefers them to people. But he's seen stuff in the forest he wasn't meant to. I just know it. He's been hit a couple of times in the head. Hit bad, with a club. Someone came from behind a tree. Least I think that was what happened. It was all I could get out of him. They'd have to do something like that to get him, cos he's strong. He got away both times, but I reckon it was attempted murder.'

'So that business with the fox,' said Maya, 'when McMurdo and Bryn went after him—'

'He just found it,' said Bonny. 'Then panicked and ran off. He gets upset when he sees dead animals, specially if they've been cut up.'

'Is it Zep?' said Maya. 'Behind all this?'

'Don't know.'

Maya turned to Mo.

'Is it Zep?' she said. 'Who's doing all this bad stuff?'

'He won't answer you,' said Bonny.

Maya took no notice.

'Mo? Is it Zep? Give a nod if it's yes. Or move your hand or something. If it's yes.'

'It won't work,' said Bonny.

She was right. The boy just stood there, the half-drunk bottle in one hand, the silver foil from the pie in the other. The confusion in his face turned to fear as Maya went on watching him.

'I'm sorry, Mo,' she said quickly. 'I didn't mean to upset you.'

Bonny stepped past her and looked into Mo's face.

'Put the top back on the bottle,' she said. 'That's it. Now put the bottle in the rucksack. Now the silver foil. No, no, leave the apple pie. You're having that another time. We're walking Maya back to The Rowan Tree.'

And a few moments later they were cutting across the fields. Bonny and Maya walked side by side, Mo bumbling behind them with the rucksack. Bonny was silent, and Maya was glad of it. She had no wish to speak. She just wanted to get home.

The moonlight was bright upon the land. She stared about her as she walked, recognizing nothing. She must have run this way but it was still unfamiliar. It was some distance too. She found it hard to believe she'd covered so much ground. The only familiar thing was the shoulder of the forest, now over to the right.

She stared uneasily at it.

They reached the stile into the pasture that led up to The Rowan Tree and Bonny stopped.

'You can do the rest on your own.'

Maya gazed into the long grass beyond. The Rowan Tree

was just out of view from here and so were the bushes by the buried body. She felt a sudden fear of this last short stretch. But she knew Bonny would come no further.

'Thanks, Bonny,' she said.

'Not a word, OK?' said Bonny. 'About me and Mo.'

'I promise.'

'Because if people find out where Mo is, someone nasty'll come for him, right? He could get killed. And it'll be your fault.'

Maya looked over at the boy, standing woodenly nearby.

'Goodbye, Mo,' she called.

The boy shifted on his feet. She turned to Bonny again.

'I won't tell anyone.'

'Make sure you don't.'

And Bonny set off the way they had come. Mo stood there for a moment, watching Maya. Bonny called over her shoulder.

'Come on, big guy.'

And the boy turned and followed. Maya watched them disappear, then climbed over the stile and set off through the long grass towards The Rowan Tree. It was still hidden from view by the slope and she could feel her heart racing again.

Zep could easily reappear. He'd hidden in the long grass before. He could leap out in front of her, block the way back, and it could all start again. He could even kill her here without anyone seeing it.

Then she caught sight of The Rowan Tree. There were lights on in all the windows. She started to run. More lights appeared, over to the left, and now she could see police cars in the lane—and torches.

Where the body was buried.

17

The lounge at The Rowan Tree. Mum's arm round her on the sofa, Dad and Tom sitting to the left, DI Henderson and DC Coker to the right, Annie Shaw directly in front. Maya looked back at her.

She knew what the policewoman was here for. She'd been kept out of the interview last time but DI Henderson had clearly decided the wayward girl from The Rowan Tree needed special female support.

Maya frowned. She'd have preferred another female. There were too many associations with Annie Shaw; and for all the woman's friendliness, she was being subtly persistent.

'OK, Maya,' she said. 'I know this is very distressing, but I just want to go through everything again to make sure we've got all the details right.'

'I think Maya's told you all she can,' said Mum.

'Even so,' said the policewoman.

She looked at Maya.

'Is that all right? Can we go through it again?'

Maya said nothing. From outside the window came the sounds of the forensic team and the other police officers busy at the site of the buried body. There were voices in the lane too. She listened to them. People from the village probably, even though this was still the middle of the night. She was sure she could hear McMurdo asking questions over the wall. So by breakfast time everyone in

Hembury would know about the body found outside The Rowan Tree—and the latest piece of craziness from the Munro girl.

Annie Shaw smiled.

'I tell you what, Maya, let me do the talking this time and you tell me if I've got anything wrong. How about that?'

'OK.'

'So,' said the policewoman, 'you were sleeping with your mum, in your mum and dad's room. You heard a sound outside the window. You looked out and noticed that some digging had been going on in the pasture. You didn't see anybody there but you went out to investigate. Right so far?'

'Yes,' said Maya.

'Sure?'

'Yes.'

'OK,' said Annie. 'You got a torch and spade and you went out to look.'

Maya felt the silence deepen around her.

'Yes,' she said.

'That's what happened, is it?'

'Yes.'

'You didn't wake your mum and dad?'

'No.'

'Why not?'

'I told you earlier,' said Maya, 'I just—'

'Didn't want to wake them.'

'Yes.'

'Because they haven't been sleeping well lately,' said Annie. 'You didn't want to bother them. Is that right?'

'Yes.'

'What about Tom?' said Annie. 'You didn't think of waking him?'

'No.'

'Has he been sleeping badly too?'

'I don't know . . . I suppose I just . . . didn't do it.'

She glanced at Tom and saw his lips tight together.

'All right,' said Annie. 'You went out into the pasture, found the spot by the bushes, prodded about with the spade and saw a dead fox's head, and then a human foot sticking out of the ground. But before you could run to The Rowan Tree to get help, Zep appeared in this . . . fox costume.'

'Yes.'

DI Henderson shifted in his chair. Annie Shaw glanced at him, then back at Maya.

'So you dropped the torch and spade,' she went on, 'which was just as well—'

'Why?' said Maya.

'Because when your parents realized you were missing and called us out, we saw the light of the torch from the window and it showed us where you'd been. And where the body was. Anyway, you dropped the torch and spade, and Zep chased you across the fields. And then he disappeared. Have I got that right?'

'Yes,' said Maya.

'And you can't remember where you ended up?'

'No.'

Annie leaned forward.

'So Zep didn't attack you?'

'He . . . '

'He what?'

'He . . . confronted me.'

'Confronted you?'

Maya tried to think. There had to be some way she could report Zep's behaviour without breaking her word to Bonny and telling them about Mo.

'He came right up close,' she said, 'and he went on about me . . . giving him a good time, and then he pushed himself against me, and . . . and I told him to leave me alone but he caught my shoulder and—'

'Hold on,' said DI Henderson. 'You told us earlier that he ran after you and then disappeared. Now you're saying he confronted you and tried to grab you.'

'By the dead body.'

She looked from face to face, desperate to make the story work.

'I meant by the dead body,' she said. 'By the bushes. That's where he confronted me and . . . did all that. So I ran off and he chased after me. And I must have lost him, because he disappeared.'

She saw Tom shaking his head.

'What's happened to you, sis?' he muttered.

'Tommy—'

'You never used to do things like this. First you run off into the forest and see bodies that aren't there.'

'They were there.'

'The police didn't find anything. And now you've run off again.'

'Well, there's a body this time,' said Maya. She looked at DI Henderson. 'Isn't there?'

'Yes, Maya,' said the officer. 'There's a body this time.'

'It doesn't make any difference,' said Tom, scowling at her. 'You never used to do this kind of stuff. And you never used to lie either.'

'Tom,' said Mum. 'Ease up.'

The door opened and WPC Becket walked in.

'Sir?' she said, looking at DI Henderson.

The officer walked over to the door, exchanged a few words, then returned to his chair.

'We have a confirmed identification of the body,' he

122

said. 'I'm afraid it wasn't easy, given the nature of the injuries sustained.'

He took a slow breath.

'But I'm not prepared to go into details here.'

Maya shivered. She could guess what the details were. She pictured the effigy, the figures carved in the trees, the mutilated foxes—and tried to push the images away.

'Can you give us the name of the dead person?' said Dad. 'Or is that not allowed?'

'It's allowed in this case,' said DI Henderson, 'because I'd like to discuss the deceased with you.'

'So who was it?' said Dad.

'A Mrs Rebecca Flint.'

DI Henderson turned to Maya.

'Did you know her?'

'What are you asking Maya for?' said Mum.

'No particular reason,' said the officer. 'But I'm guessing Maya might have met Mrs Flint. Or indeed the rest of you. Since there's a connection.'

'I don't know of any connection,' said Dad.

'Dad,' said Maya, 'Mrs Flint and her husband owned The Rowan Tree before we did. He walked out on her but she stayed on in the village. Jake told me about it. I saw Mrs Flint a couple of days ago outside the church. She walked back with me to The Rowan Tree.'

Tom grunted.

'You might be the last person who saw her alive.'

'I wasn't,' she said.

'So who was?'

Maya glared at him.

'The person who killed her.'

She felt a ripple of tension run round the room.

'Can you remember anything important,' said DI Henderson, 'from your conversation with Mrs Flint?'

'She told me to be careful.'

'Careful of what?'

'Just careful.'

'Hm.'

The policeman looked round at his colleagues.

'There is one obvious lead with Mrs Flint,' he said. 'If Hembury gossip's anything to go by.'

The other officers nodded.

'What does that mean?' said Dad.

But none of them answered this. DI Henderson stood up.

'I think for the moment we'll leave you to get your breath back,' he said, 'and give Maya the support she needs. I should warn you, however, that it's very likely we're going to want to ask her some more questions. And possibly the rest of you.'

'We're happy to co-operate in any way we can,' said Dad.

'Thank you, sir.'

'Are you going to bring Zep in?' said Mum.

'We've got to find him first,' said DI Henderson. 'But yes, we're certainly going to want to speak to him. Which brings me to a final point.'

He looked round at them all.

'It would help very much if you would undertake not to leave the premises until further notice. That particularly applies to you, Maya. Do you understand?'

'Maya's not going anywhere,' said Mum. 'She's grounded.'

'I'd like you all to be grounded,' said DI Henderson. 'I'm requesting that you stay here. It's for your own safety. The murderer is still at large. How many other people are living at The Rowan Tree right now?'

'None,' said Dad.

'No guests?'

Dad glanced at Mum, then back at the officer.

'Not at the moment,' he said.

'Any staff live on the premises?'

'No.'

'So it's just the four of you here?'

'Yes.'

DI Henderson pulled on his coat.

'We'll try to keep busybodies away but you'd better be prepared for a bit of unwanted attention. The pasture area will be cordoned off and nobody will be allowed there without police permission, and that includes all of you. In the meantime, I'd advise you to stay inside The Rowan Tree, keep all windows and doors locked, and take real care over who you allow onto the premises.'

'We can still trade, can't we?' said Dad. 'I mean, we've got to run our business.'

'We can't stop you trading,' said DI Henderson, 'but if you want my honest opinion, it would be one less thing for the police to worry about if you did.'

'But why?' said Mum. 'How can our business affect your investigation?'

'Put it this way,' said the policeman. 'It seems to me that when a former owner of The Rowan Tree turns up dead in the pasture nearby, and the daughter of the present owners—how shall I put it?—keeps getting into trouble, then something's pointing to this place.'

DI Henderson gave them a nod.

'Thank you for your time.'

And the officers left the room. But almost at once the door opened again and Annie Shaw slipped back in.

'Yes?' said Mum.

'I know this is a bad time, Mrs Munro,' she said, 'but Bryn and I have got a table booked for this evening. I presume you'd like us to cancel it?'

'You don't have to,' said Mum.

'We don't want to,' said Annie. 'The Rowan Tree's a special place for us. We had our first ever date here, and I think Bryn wants to ask me something important later, if you know what I mean. But obviously I'm thinking with all that's going on, the last thing you want—'

'We need all the business we can get right now,' said Mum. 'You and Bryn are more than welcome to eat here.'

'Of course,' said Dad. 'We'll be delighted to serve you.'

'Thank you,' said Annie. 'Thank you so much.'

'Don't come,' said Maya.

She looked down, pictures of the forest drifting through her mind. Among them, Annie's face.

'Don't come,' she said again.

She felt Mum stand up, usher the policewoman to the door, talking low. But the words came whispering back.

'Maya's very upset. I'm sure you understand.'

'Of course.'

'The table will be ready. We look forward to seeing you.'

Maya closed her eyes. But the pictures of the forest grew stronger.

18

The big bed again, Mum beside her. Maya lay rigid. She knew she was in disgrace with the family. No one had said so, not even Tom, but it was obvious what they thought. She listened to the sound of Dad and Tom wandering about upstairs.

'I'm sure they don't need to check up there,' said Mum. 'They've done the ground floor and the first floor rooms. They don't need to do any more.'

Maya said nothing. As far as she was concerned, Dad and Tom couldn't check The Rowan Tree enough. Mum reached out and pulled her close.

'I'm not angry with you,' she said.

'You are,' said Maya. 'So's Dad. So's Tommy.'

'That's not true.'

'Tommy's mad at me.'

'No, he's not,' said Mum. 'He's worried about you and it's unsettled him. That's why he flew off the handle earlier. I wish he hadn't done it in front of the police, but there you go. That's Tom. You know what he's like. Something gets inside his head and the next moment it's coming out of his mouth. But he's not angry with you. None of us are. We're just very concerned about you.'

Maya listened. 'They've gone quiet up there,' she said.

'Don't worry,' said Mum. 'We'll hear them again soon.'

And sure enough, the footsteps returned, heading up the stairs to the attic room.

'What on earth are they going up there for?' said Mum. 'No one's going to break in at the top of the building. Ah, well. Let's hope they settle after that and we can get some sleep.'

She yawned.

'Maya, listen. We're really not angry with you, OK? We're just worried. And very confused. Because this kind of behaviour isn't like you.'

'I'm sorry,' said Maya.

'And with a murderer now on the loose, I can't have you running off again.'

'I know,' said Maya. 'I won't. I promise.'

'You promised that before,' said Mum.

More sounds from above: steps coming down from the attic; then they split, as Tom headed to his room, Dad to Room Seven. A few moments later, all was quiet. Maya went on listening.

No sounds from The Rowan Tree, none from the lane. She breathed slowly out. There was only one sound she was listening for. She almost hoped it would come, so that Mum would hear it too, and then believe her.

But there was no scratching on the door.

Mum kissed her.

'Going to tell me now?' she said. 'What really happened?'

Maya thought of Bonny, and Mo, and her promise.

'It wasn't the truth, was it?' said Mum. 'What you told the police. Maybe some of it was, but most of it wasn't. We all knew it. Dad, Tom, and I knew it, because we know you so well, but the police weren't fooled either.'

Mum paused.

'And I think the only reason they didn't push you harder was because they could see you were traumatized after what you'd been through. Whatever that was.'

Maya started to cry.

'Sweetheart,' said Mum, 'no one doubts something dreadful happened to you. And I'm sure you weren't lying about that awful boy Zep. The sooner the police get hold of him the better. But we could all see you weren't telling us what really happened.'

'I can't,' said Maya. 'I just can't . . . say any more.'

'Even to me?'

Maya went on crying.

'OK,' said Mum. 'It's OK.'

'It's not OK,' said Maya. 'I'm being horrible.'

'You're not being horrible,' said Mum. 'You're scared out of your wits. That's what's making you feel like this. You're not being horrible at all.'

They lay there together, neither speaking, and Maya finally stopped crying.

'Mum?' she said.

'Yes, love.'

'I did see those bodies in the forest.'

'I'm sure you did.'

'I know you think I imagined them, but I didn't.'

Mum kissed her again.

'I've been wondering,' she said.

'Wondering what?' said Maya.

'If this has got something to do with your problem with Annie Shaw and her boyfriend.'

'I don't understand.'

'I think you do,' said Mum. 'You don't want them to come and eat here later. I've been trying to work out why. But then I remembered how you said the man you saw lying in the forest had red hair. And hasn't this Bryn character got red hair? I'm sure Milly mentioned that he has.'

Maya didn't answer.

'Hasn't he?' said Mum.

'Yes.'

'So is that it?' said Mum. 'You're worried about this man because he's got red hair? Or is it Annie Shaw? Have you got a thing about her? She seems nice to me.'

'She is nice.'

'So is it Bryn? Is he the problem? You met him. What's he like?'

'He's nice too.'

'Then why don't you want them to come and eat here? The Rowan Tree's a special place for them. Annie said so. They had their first date here. And he's got something important he wants to ask her over dinner. So I guess that means he's going to pop the question. And we need the money. Maya, everybody wins. So what's your problem with them coming here?'

Maya pictured the forest again: the clearing, the bodies.

The eyes of the fox, drawing her.

She could feel the animal close again.

'I just don't want them to come,' she said.

Mum gave a long sigh.

'Well, we can't stop them coming just because you don't want them to. We've got to have a better reason than that. And so far you haven't given us one. Because you haven't told us anything.'

'I just . . .'

But Maya fell silent. It was no good. Mum would never believe her if she described what she'd really seen in the forest. It still didn't seem possible that Annie and Bryn could have been lying there dead. And yet . . .

Perhaps the picture had a different meaning.

An even more sinister one.

If that was true, then she already knew what Annie and Bryn would be wearing for their dinner date later.

Only one thing would be missing: the horseshoe pendant. She suddenly found herself hoping it would remain so. If the pendant stayed lost, then surely the picture couldn't be complete.

Couldn't possibly happen.

If that was what this really meant.

Mum whispered to her.

'Try not to worry. Everything's going to be all right. I promise it is. They'll catch the murderer and sort out whatever's going on. And this other stuff that's upsetting you, that'll be OK too. You're going to be fine.'

She started to sing. The old familiar song.

'But surely you see my lady, out in the garden there . . .'

'You've jumped to the end of the song,' said Maya.

'Poetic licence,' said Mum.

And she sang on.

'Rivalling the glittering sunshine, with a glory of golden hair.'

She stroked the top of Maya's head.

'I always think of that as your song.'

'But I haven't got golden hair,' said Maya.

'You have when I sing this song.'

'Your hair's more golden than mine is.'

'It's more grey too,' said Mum.

They fell silent again, holding each other.

'You're listening for something,' said Mum. 'What is it?'

'Just listening.'

'Oh, Maya,' said Mum. 'So many mysteries.'

'What do you mean?'

'So many things you can't tell me.'

Maya hesitated.

'I was listening for the scratching sound on the door. I told you about it. And Doctor Wade. That time I screamed. None of you believed me. But I heard it. And that's what I was listening for.'

'Have you heard it again?' said Mum.

'Not tonight.'

'I'm glad. Come here. I want to give you a hug.'

Maya clung to her, eyes closed, and somehow she fell asleep. But it was not for long. She woke suddenly, fear churning inside her, though she didn't know why. Mum was asleep, arms still round her. All was dark and still.

She let her eyes run round the room. Nothing unusual, no sounds in the night. Her eyes went on searching. No trace of dawn in the window. She felt an urge to look behind her but that meant twisting her body round and she didn't want to pull back from Mum or take her eyes from the area round the door.

Because something had definitely woken her, and she sensed it had come from there. The stillness in the room remained. She pressed herself closer to Mum but kept her eyes moving. Just the same shadowy features: the dressing table, the chair, the wardrobe, the chest of drawers.

The door.

And there it was.

Scratch, scratch.

Silence.

Mum stirred but didn't wake. Maya clutched her.

'Mum,' she whispered, 'it's out there.'

Mum murmured something, but went on sleeping.

The silence continued. Maya listened hard. This had to be wrong. Dad and Tom had checked all the rooms, locked the doors and windows.

'Mum,' she said, and this time Mum woke.

'Maya?'

'I heard the noise,' she said. 'The scratching on the door. I heard it.'

'How long ago?'

'Just a moment.'

Mum climbed out of bed and started towards the door.

'Mum, no.'

'It's all right,' said Mum.

She pulled open the door and stood there, looking out. Maya stared nervously after her. Mum switched on the corridor light and stepped out.

'Mum,' called Maya, 'don't leave me.'

Mum glanced round at her.

'I can't see anything strange. But I can check if you want. You just curl up in bed. Dive under the sheets and burrow down. I won't be long. I'll close the door on you. You'll be quite safe.'

'Mum, please.'

Mum studied her face for a few moments, then smiled.

'OK.'

She switched off the corridor light, closed the door and climbed back into bed.

'I don't think there's anything nasty out there,' she said.

'I did hear it.'

'I thought you were asleep. You dropped off before I did. I felt you.'

Mum pulled her close again.

'Come on,' she said. 'Let's have another go.'

They lay there and after a few minutes Mum fell asleep again. But Maya did not. She curled up under the duvet and stared out over the top, listening as before; and the night moved on, in silence.

19

Morning brought the police back, and a new form of attention.

'Just what we need,' muttered Dad, peering out of the bedroom window. 'The press.'

Maya and Mum peered out too.

'The police are keeping them back,' said Mum.

'Makes no difference,' said Dad. 'We're still going to be all over the bloody news. The Rowan Tree and a dead body. All in the same sentence. Going to be great for business.'

Maya stared down. The lane seemed filled with cameras and microphones. Several of the locals were there too, packed in among the reporters. She could see McMurdo speaking to one of them. A row of police officers guarded the entrance to The Rowan Tree. So far no one had rung the bell but this looked about to change.

WPC Becket and another policewoman were approaching the front door.

'Here we go,' said Dad, and he set off downstairs.

Maya felt an arm slip round her shoulder.

'You're grounded, remember?' said Mum. 'No going outside.'

'OK.'

Mum squeezed her arm.

'Try not to worry. You'll be safe here.'

Maya frowned. She didn't feel safe anywhere now. The

village, the fields, the forest—all seemed threatening; but The Rowan Tree felt more threatening still. Something stalked the hotel, something she couldn't see. It haunted the rooms, hers most of all, and it scratched its presence upon the doors, and upon her.

She felt the fox again, somewhere near.

'Go away,' she whispered to it.

'What's that, darling?' said Mum.

Maya turned to face the door.

'What is it?' said Mum.

'Something's out there. In the corridor.'

'I don't think so.'

'I heard a shuffling sound.'

But all was quiet now.

'I definitely heard something,' said Maya.

'Probably your dad coming back up.'

'He's still downstairs. Talking to those policewomen. I can hear him.'

Mum listened for a moment.

'You're right,' she said. 'I'll check the corridor for you.'

She walked over to the bedroom door.

'I'm sure it's nothing,' she said.

Maya watched, warily. Mum opened the door and pointed to the empty corridor.

'See?'

'There was definitely something out there.'

Mum put her head round the door, then suddenly called out.

'What are you doing skulking there?'

From outside came the shuffle of footsteps. Then Mum gave a laugh.

'It's OK,' she said. 'I was only joking.'

Tom's face appeared in the doorway. Maya glanced at him. He was watching her strangely, as though he wasn't sure what to say. She turned back to the window and saw a small film crew gathering round DI Henderson. From the doorway came the sound of Mum whispering to Tom.

'Go easy on her, OK? No more outbursts like yesterday.'

She felt the words move in her mouth, as if by themselves.

'Someone's going to die.'

There was a silence, then Tom spoke.

'Someone's already died. Rebecca Flint's died.'

'Someone else,' said Maya.

She heard footsteps draw close, felt Mum take her hand.

'Come on,' said Mum. 'Let's eat.'

She remembered little of breakfast. She was aware of not being hungry, of picking at her food; Mum fussing round, Tom keeping his distance, the voices of the police-women out in the hall, talking to Dad.

They hadn't asked to speak to her yet.

Then suddenly she heard the front door open and close. She walked over to the window and stared out. The two women were wandering down the lane, talking to DC Coker. She saw eyes turn towards her and a moment later cameras started to flash.

Dad spoke from the doorway.

'Draw the curtains, Maya. We don't want people gawp-ing in at us.'

She looked round, startled.

'I didn't hear you come in,' she said.

'Just draw the curtains,' he said.

She pulled them across and sat down at the breakfast table. Mum stood up.

'Coffee, anyone?'

'Maybe later,' said Dad.

Mum sat down again.

'So what did the police want?' she said. 'I thought they'd be asking to speak to Maya again.'

'They did want to speak to Maya again,' said Dad. 'But I told them it'll have to wait. I said she's too upset to talk right now and unless it's absolutely essential to the investigation, I'd rather they gave her a few more hours. And preferably another day. Just to collect herself a bit. They seemed OK with that.'

'Is Maya a murder suspect?' said Tom.

'No, no,' said Dad. 'Zep's the one they're looking for.'

'Have they found him?'

'Not yet.'

'So is there any news?' said Mum.

'They just repeated what they told us last night,' said Dad. 'Only with a bit more detail. Which I'm not going to go into.'

'Why not?' said Tom.

'Because it's not very pleasant,' said Dad. 'I imagine it'll be on the news later—or an edited version will—so you can catch it then if you really want to. They've confirmed it was the body of Rebecca Flint. The lady who owned The Rowan Tree before we did. And let's just say . . . ' Dad hesitated. 'It seems to have been some kind of . . . ritualistic murder.'

'Now I'm making coffee,' said Mum.

She stood up, switched on the kettle, then turned and looked back at them.

'Maybe we're all suspects.'

'I doubt it,' said Dad. 'Like I just said, Zep's the one they really want to find. WPC Becket made that clear. But she did say they're going to want to ask more questions.'

The doorbell rang.

'Talk of the devil,' said Mum. 'I'm making coffee, whatever happens. You can let the police in.'

137

But it wasn't the police who entered the kitchen. It was Milly, Roxy, and Jake. Maya gazed up at them, only half-seeing.

'You don't look good, sweetheart,' said Milly.

Maya closed her eyes, unable to look at her. Or any of them.

'It's OK, Maya,' said Jake.

She opened her eyes again. He was standing there oddly and it took her a moment to realize he was close to tears.

'Tough times,' said Milly.

She turned to Mum.

'We'll get to work straight away. We're all cut up about Mrs Flint. She was good to us when we worked here. We'll be happier being busy, so since there's no guests right now, I suggest the three of us get cleaning. Is that kettle on for coffee?'

'Yes,' said Mum.

'Roxy'll make that for you. All right, girl?'

'I'll do it,' said Roxy.

'Have some with us,' said Mum.

'We won't, if you don't mind,' said Milly. 'We'd rather get stuck in and have a break later. Jake, I suggest you start in the dining room, then do the conservatory and the lounge.'

Jake didn't move. Maya looked at him. He was watching her and the pain was still in his face.

'What was going on, Jake?' she said.

He didn't answer.

'DI Henderson said something,' she went on, 'about Hembury gossip.'

'That's true,' said Mum. 'And he made it sound important.'

Roxy looked up from the coffee cups but said nothing.

'Jake knows about it,' said Maya.

Jake glanced at Mum.

'Can I sit down, Mrs Munro? Is that all right?'

'Of course it is.'

He sat down at the table opposite Maya.

'You don't have to talk about this, Jake,' said Mum, 'if it's something distressing. And it's maybe none of our business.'

Jake shrugged. 'Everyone knows about it now.'

'About what?' said Tom.

'Zep and Mrs Flint.'

Tom stared at him.

'Are you telling me—'

'Yeah,' said Jake. 'I am.'

'But Zep's only about nineteen,' said Tom. 'And Mrs Flint must be—'

'Over forty,' said Jake. 'Yeah, she is.' He frowned. 'Was.'

'Bloody hell,' said Tom.

'It probably started out innocent,' said Milly. 'I reckon she took pity on him. Rough kid, roaming about, nobody wanting nothing to do with him. Apart from the girls. Stupid fools.'

'But the age difference,' said Mum.

'Like I say,' said Milly, 'it probably started out innocent. He was never living nowhere settled. Nowhere you could find him. Not that anyone was looking. But he'd disappear for weeks, then turn up and cause trouble. He's a nasty piece of work, no question. But he probably looked hungry and lost and she felt sorry for him.'

'So is Jake right,' said Dad, 'and everyone knew about this?'

'Don't know about everyone,' said Milly, 'but they was always talking about it in The Rose and Crown and the village shop. Good story for people who like smut, I guess. Mr and Mrs Flint split up, he goes off with someone else, she moves out of The Rowan Tree but buys another place in the village, and pretty soon after she's letting Zep doss in her outhouse.'

'But dossing in the outhouse is one thing,' said Mum. 'It doesn't mean—'

'That came later,' said Jake.

He looked down at the table.

'I liked Mrs Flint,' he said. 'I know people thought she was a snob, but she was OK, more than OK. She always treated me and Roxy right. Stood up for us when her husband got snotty. But she must have been . . . '

He took a slow breath.

'She must have been so lonely. And I don't suppose she felt very attractive after Mr Flint went off with that woman from Cresswell. I guess Zep was kind of exciting and risky and she wanted to have a bit of fun, just for a while probably. But I knew it was going to be bad for her when he started sleeping there. I just didn't know it was going to be this bad.'

He looked up again.

'And now things are going to get worse.'

He fixed his eyes on Maya.

'Aren't they?'

20

She stared at her bedroom door. It stood there like a senti-nel, blocking her way. She faced it, her mind on the space beyond. She ought to go in. She knew that. Break her fear. It was only a room. Just grip the handle, turn, push, enter. It should be simple.

But her hand stayed where it was.

She listened to the voices outside The Rowan Tree. The press and locals seemed to have moved—or been moved— further down the lane towards the village square. Inside the hotel she heard no voices at all, just the drone of a vacuum cleaner at the other end of the building.

At least no one had objected when she'd said she wanted to be alone in her room. She'd been worried Tom might offer to come with her, or even insist. But he was still keeping his distance, still wary of her.

She felt so frightened now: of all that had happened, and all that was yet to come. She thought of Annie and Bryn, due to arrive in just a few hours, saw them lying dead in the forest, and then the other two figures she'd glimpsed at the top of the clearing, hazy in the dusk: one sprawled upon the ground, the other standing over it.

Who were they? And what part did they have to play in all this?

She heard footsteps behind her and turned.

Jake was standing there.

'I'm sorry,' he said. 'I thought you were in your room.'

141

'I was just about to go in.'

'Milly sent me to get some stuff from the broom cupboard.'

'You've gone past the broom cupboard.'

'I know.'

They stood there in silence for a while, each watching the other.

'Thing is,' said Jake eventually, 'I came on here to see if you're all right.'

'I'm fine.'

'OK,' said Jake. 'If you say so.'

'I told everyone I wanted to be on my own,' she said.

'I know. I heard.'

'So what would you have done if I'd been inside the room?'

'I'd have knocked.'

'Would you?'

'Yeah.' Jake paused. 'Well, I might have.'

Maya said nothing.

'So . . . ' Jake hesitated. 'How come you're not in your room?'

'I told you,' she said. 'I was just about to go in.'

'OK.'

She glanced at the door, then back at Jake. He showed no sign of moving off.

'I'll get on, then,' he said.

'Thanks for looking out for me.'

'Maya?'

She studied his face. The pain was still there but he was angry too.

'I'm sorry about Rebecca Flint,' she said. 'I know you really liked her.'

'You never answered my question,' he said.

'What question?'

'The one I asked you downstairs.'

Once again she saw the figures in the forest.

And now the fox prowling round them.

'I said things are going to get worse,' said Jake. 'And then I looked at you and said, "Aren't they?" And you didn't answer.'

Still the figures in the forest—and now the horseshoe pendant: the one thing that was missing, that might just save things. If the picture meant what she feared.

'So are you going to answer?' said Jake.

'I don't know the answer.'

'But you know something.'

'I don't know who's behind the murder,' she said. 'Or the other stuff.'

'You still know something.'

'I know I'm scared,' she said. 'I know I hear things and see things no one else does. I suppose that means I'm off my head.'

'You're not off your head,' said Jake. 'But you are scared. And I shouldn't be pushing you. I'm sorry.'

The drone of the vacuum cleaner ceased; then started again a moment later.

'That's Roxy,' said Jake. 'I better get on. I'm meant to be working too.'

'Thanks for bothering about me,' said Maya.

Jake turned to go, then stopped and looked back at her.

'You do know something,' he said. 'I wish you'd trust me and tell me.'

'I do trust you.'

'But you won't tell me.'

She said nothing. He clenched a fist, knocked it softly against the wall.

'Don't be angry with me,' she said.

'I'm not angry with you. I'm angry with someone else.'

'Who?'

'The person who killed Mrs Flint,' he said.

And he disappeared down the corridor. She heard him stop at the broom cupboard, rummage inside, close the door, head downstairs, and then his steps were gone. She stared at the bedroom door again, willing herself to open it, but it was no good. She turned, leaned her back against it, and let herself slide down to the floor.

An hour passed, two. No one came along the corridor. She listened hard. There were few sounds to be heard over Roxy's vacuum cleaner, which had now moved to the ground floor, but then she caught it—clear and close.

Not the scratching she'd expected.

But the growl.

She sat up, gazed round. Nothing moved in this part of the corridor. But she sensed where the sound had come from. She twisted her head round and stared at the door. Another growl, definitely from the direction of her room.

She jumped up, her eyes on the door.

'Leave me alone,' she muttered.

She backed away from the door, still watching it. From downstairs came the sound of Dad's voice calling towards the kitchen.

'I'll just check if Maya wants some lunch.'

She hurried down the corridor to the head of the stairs. Dad was already halfway up. He caught sight of her and stopped.

'I was just coming up to see you,' he said.

She ran down and joined him.

'Have they found Zep?' she said.

'Not yet,' said Dad. 'I just had a word with DC Coker. He said they're looking everywhere but no sign of him so far. Don't worry. I'm sure they'll get him. Do you want some lunch?'

'I'm not hungry.'

'Your mum's made some soup. It's lovely. I just had some.'

'I don't really want anything.'

'But you've got to eat,' said Dad. 'You hardly touched your breakfast. I don't want you missing lunch as well. Is it because you want to be on your own today? Up in your room?'

She nodded. It seemed best to lie.

'I thought so,' said Dad. 'That's why we've left you alone. We do understand, you know, Mum and I. You want some time to yourself after all this drama, so you can get your head straight. And that's fine with us. Just so long as we know you're not going to go outside The Rowan Tree, OK?'

'OK.'

'But I still don't want you not eating,' he said. 'What if I make you some sandwiches to take back to your room?'

'Thanks,' she said.

'Come on, then,' said Dad. 'Let's do them together.'

And he set off down the stairs.

'Dad?' she called.

He stopped and looked back.

'Can I stay here?' she said.

He looked at her for a few moments, then smiled.

'Course you can. I understand. Not in the mood for talking. You wait here. I'll be back in a few minutes.'

And he was.

'Thanks, Dad,' she said.

He didn't answer. He simply handed her the sandwiches, kissed her, and was gone. She stared after him, fighting the urge to cry, then turned and made her way back to the first floor and down the corridor again.

But not to her room.

She stopped outside Room Ten and listened. All was

145

quiet. She opened the door and peeped in. Clean, tidy, made up. It would do. She stepped inside, closed the door behind her and walked round to the far side of the room; then she lay down on the floor, eased herself under the bed and cried.

When the tears stopped, the growl started again.

It seemed to seep from the walls, the floor, the ceiling. She curled up, put a hand over each ear, but the growl went on. She took her hands away, curled up even more, closed her eyes. Under the lids she saw the gaze of the fox.

'What do you want?' she murmured.

The animal went on peering into her.

'Am I your prey?' she said.

The growl faded into nothing.

And the fox with it.

She opened her eyes again and looked about her. The sandwiches lay on the floor beside her. She pulled them to her, ate them, then lay back on the floor, staring up at the underside of the bed. A dark, discomforting sleep fell over her.

She woke to the sound of voices.

Downstairs.

She rolled from under the bed and pulled herself up so that she was sitting against the wall. The voices came again, moving in the direction of the dining room. She stared at her watch. It couldn't possibly be so late.

She stood up, dropped the sandwich wrapping in the bin, walked to the door, stepped out. The corridor was silent. She found it hard to believe no one had come looking for her during the afternoon. Mum and Dad had clearly decided to give her all the time she wanted alone.

But she wasn't alone.

She knew that for certain.

146

She was being hunted.

She walked to the head of the stairs. More voices from below: Milly's this time, then Mum's, then the other voices, the ones she recognized and didn't want to hear. She walked down the stairs to the ground floor. From the kitchen came the smell of beef casserole, chicken broth, garlic bread.

She walked on, into the reception area. The lane outside was quiet now, the early evening light soft upon it. She continued towards the kitchen, the smell of the food stronger, more delectable. The voices were louder too, as though the whole household had turned out to welcome the only two customers to visit The Rowan Tree today.

And there they were in the dining room, sitting at Table Four.

21

Bryn and Annie: the last people in the world she wanted to see. Roxy was carrying them drinks on a tray, Jake handing out menus, Dad lighting candles. She stood in the doorway and watched.

It was just as she'd expected. They were wearing the clothes she'd seen in the forest: Bryn the suit, white shirt, and tie; Annie the blue dress with the low neckline, her hair tumbling over it. But there was no pendant.

She walked closer, to make doubly sure.

Definitely no pendant.

She tried to tell herself that this was good, that the picture she'd seen in the forest couldn't happen without it; but everything still felt wrong. Bryn and Annie shouldn't be here. She knew it. They shouldn't even be in each other's company.

It was too dangerous for them.

And for others.

She looked at Bryn. He seemed awkward and out of place. He kept fiddling with his cuffs and tweaking his tie. His red hair was unkempt and the slovenliness of it clashed with the formality of his suit. But Annie was clearly relaxed. She caught sight of Maya and smiled.

'Hello, Maya,' she said.

Maya stopped, well back from the table.

'No need to be nervous,' said Annie. 'I'm not here to ask you any more questions.'

Maya frowned.

'Don't be worried,' said the policewoman. 'Please don't be. I mean, check out this dress—do I really look like I'm on duty?'

'You'd better not be,' said Bryn.

'You shouldn't have come,' said Maya.

'Sweetheart,' said Dad, 'not this again.'

'You shouldn't have come,' she said. 'You and Bryn. It's too dangerous.'

'Maya,' said Jake. He moved closer to her. 'What's going to happen?'

She looked at him.

'What's going to happen?' he said.

'I don't know.'

She looked back at Annie and Bryn.

'I just know something's terribly wrong.'

Dad stepped between her and the table.

'Nothing's wrong,' he said, 'and nothing's going to happen. Except that these two are going to have a lovely meal.'

He turned to Annie and Bryn.

'I'm so sorry about this. Please don't let it spoil the evening.'

Maya stood there, unsure what to say or do. Nobody seemed to be taking any more notice of her. Dad was bent over the table, talking Bryn and Annie through the menu options; Roxy had bustled off to the kitchen. But Jake was still watching her.

He walked slowly up to her.

'Please tell me you believe me,' she said.

Before he could answer, she heard Mum's voice behind her.

'Maya, I've got a job for you.'

She let herself be led through to the hall.

'I'm sorry, Mum,' she said. 'I know I'm an embarrassment.'

'You're not an embarrassment.' Mum stopped by the kitchen door and looked her in the face. 'But you are a concern. And now Tom is too.'

'What's wrong with him?'

'Nothing,' said Mum, 'if you ask him. But he would say that, wouldn't he? He's like his father, chip off the old block. He'd have to collapse before he admitted he was ill. But he looked like he was about to do just that this afternoon. While you were up in your room.'

'He collapsed?'

'I didn't say that,' said Mum. 'I said he looked like he was about to. I had to keep on at him till he finally admitted he was feeling a bit queasy. So he's gone to have a lie-down. Can you go up and check he's all right?'

'Sure,' said Maya.

'I've been looking in on him myself,' said Mum, 'and I think he's OK. He was dropping off last time I checked, and that's a good sign. But I'm busy down here now and it would help me if you could keep an eye on him. Might help you too. Take your mind off . . . well . . . '

'Myself.'

'Yes,' said Mum. 'Since you mention it. But don't wake him if he's sleeping.'

'I won't.'

Maya hurried off, fighting a new fear that was growing inside her. She reached the first floor and turned down the corridor towards Tom's room. All was silent in this part of the hotel, though she could still catch the voices below.

She stopped outside Tom's room and listened. No sound of breathing or movement within. She eased open the door and craned her head round. He was lying on the bed, still dressed, his eyes closed. 'I'm not asleep,' he murmured.

'Tommy?'

He opened his eyes.

'I thought you were Mum,' he said.

He sounded weak, looked weak.

'Can I come in?' she said.

'Yeah.'

She stepped into the room and closed the door behind her.

'Sorry I'm not Mum,' she said.

'I don't want you to be Mum,' he muttered. 'I want you to be you.'

She walked up to the bed. He didn't move but kept his eyes on her.

'You don't look good, Tommy,' she said.

'Neither do you.'

'Mum said you nearly collapsed. And you're feeling queasy.'

'I'm fine.'

He went on staring up at her, then pulled his legs into his chest.

'Are you making space for me,' she said, 'or just curling up?'

'Both, I guess.'

She sat down on the bed.

'Tommy?'

'Yeah?'

'You look really terrible. I think I'd better get Mum.'

'No.' He reached out and caught her hand. 'Don't get Mum. She'll only call the doctor.'

'But that's what you need.'

'I don't need the doctor. I just need a bit of sleep and I'll be OK.'

'Tom—'

'Sis, listen.' He squeezed her hand. 'There's something I've got to know. It's really important. I can't stop thinking about it.'

'What is it?'

'That time we went walking and you ran off into the forest and saw . . . whatever you saw . . . '

'The bodies,' she said firmly.

'You said something,' he went on. 'Before you ran off, we saw an owl hunting, and you said—'

'Someone's going to die.'

'Yes,' said Tom. 'You said that . . . and Rebecca Flint died. And then you said it again this morning. In Mum and Dad's bedroom. And you said you weren't talking about Rebecca Flint. You said you meant somebody else is going to die.'

He looked at her hard.

'Did you mean me?'

'Of course not.'

'Am I going to die?'

'Of course you're not.'

'Do you know that for certain?'

Maya hesitated.

'Yeah.'

Tom closed his eyes again.

'You're a terrible liar,' he said. 'You always were.'

'Tommy—'

'You hesitated,' he said. 'Just now. You hesitated.'

'That's only because . . . I don't know who I meant when I said someone's going to die.'

'So it could be me?'

'No, it's . . . '

She stared down at him, wishing he'd open his eyes and look at her again. But he didn't.

'Tommy,' she said, 'you're not going to die.'

Yet even as she spoke, she felt doubts welling inside her. She stared round the room, searching for shadows. There were none to be seen, but the light was growing pale.

'You still look terrible,' she said. 'I want to get Mum.'

'Don't, sis, please.'

He gripped her more tightly.

'I just . . . want you with me,' he said. 'I don't want Mum. Or Dad. They're already worried sick about you. They don't need me on their minds as well. I'll be fine, sis. I just need . . . a bit of sleep . . . and . . . '

He opened his eyes again.

'Please stay with me. Till I fall asleep. That's all. I'll feel better if you're here. Can you do that?'

'OK,' she said.

And Tom closed his eyes again.

She stayed there on the bed, holding his hand, and silence fell around them. Neither broke it, neither moved. She looked down. It was hard to tell whether Tom was falling asleep or not. She went on sitting there, aware of the sun losing its strength. Tom lay still, his knees tucked into his chest.

'I'm scared, sis,' he said suddenly.

'I know you are,' she said.

She watched him for a few more minutes, then realized he was asleep. She eased her hand free, leaned back and whispered into the silent room.

'I'm scared too, Tommy.'

She walked over to the window and looked out. The back garden still caught the remnants of the light but dusk was not far off. She stared beyond the wall towards the forest. It seemed to glower at her and she drew the curtains across.

Still silence, apart from Tom's breathing. She glanced over at him. He'd uncurled his legs but he looked distorted, not right at all, even though he was sleeping. She took a step closer to the bed, stopped, waited.

A click downstairs. Footsteps outside The Rowan Tree, voices fading. It's now, she thought. It's happening now, it's starting now. Tom groaned suddenly.

'Sis,' he muttered. 'I don't feel good.'

'I'll get Mum.'

She tore out of the room and down the stairs. But Mum was already on her way up.

'Is Tom all right?' she said.

'He needs a doctor,' said Maya.

'I've called the doctor.'

'Mum, what's going on?'

'I don't know,' said Mum, 'and now your dad's feeling ill too. Try and help him if you can. I'm off to see Tom.'

Maya ran down to the bottom of the stairs and saw Dad stumbling along the hall towards her. She hurried over and threw her arms round him.

'Easy, love,' he said. 'I'm not feeling too strong.'

She let go of him.

'What's happened?' she said.

'I don't know. I just feel queasy. It came on straight after those two left.'

'Bryn and Annie?'

'Yes,' said Dad. 'They only had a main course. I think he must have popped the question because they were tense as hell to start with and the next time we looked they were all lovey-dovey. I think they just ate up quick because they wanted to be by themselves.'

He took a hard, heavy breath.

'I think it's turned out OK for them,' he said. 'She bought him a silver watch. He put it on in front of us. I'm

154

not sure he remembered to buy her anything in return. I didn't see a ring or anything. But she's happy anyway because we found her horseshoe pendant.'

'What?' said Maya.

'We found it,' said Dad. 'Well, Roxy did. Ground floor corridor, just under your bedroom. She picked it up in the vacuum cleaner. Gave it to me and I recognized it from what Annie Shaw said, so I gave it back to her.'

'What did she do with it?'

'What do you think she did with it?' said Dad. 'She put it on in front of me, then gave me a kiss.'

Dad clapped a hand to his forehead.

'Dad, you look terrible,' she said. 'Like Tom.'

'Your mum's called the doctor.'

'I know.'

'Listen, Maya.' Dad touched her on the arm. 'I just need to have a sit-down in the lounge.'

'Dad, you look really, really bad.'

'Don't fuss over me,' he said. 'I'll be all right in a bit. Go and help your mum, OK? Milly and the others are clearing up in the dining room. You go and make sure Tom's all right.'

And Dad lurched off.

Maya turned away. This couldn't be right. The silver watch, the horseshoe pendant. She ran down the corridor, checking the ceiling as she went. Here was the spot, right underneath her room. She switched on the light and stared up. It was easy to see.

The crumbling plaster.

Just one place, and very small.

But enough for a pendant to slip through.

She sprinted back down the corridor and up the stairs. The growl was back and it was coming from one place. She ignored Tom's room and headed for her own. The

155

growl grew louder. She charged up to the door, thrust it open and burst in.

The growl stopped.

But she knew the animal was near.

She stared at the windows before her. The dying light still hung upon them. She walked up to the first and looked out: past the lane, past the square, past the church—and there they were, the two figures, hand in hand, heading for the forest.

She turned to the second window.

And saw two yellow eyes peering in.

22

'I won't come,' she said.

The eyes blinked. They were almost as high as the window itself. The fox had somehow found its way onto the roof of the garage. She stared. It must have come in through the gate at the end of the garden, slipped down the side-path, jumped up onto one of the bins, jumped again to the top of the oil tank, and again to the roof of the garage. It was now prowling up and down, its eyes throwing flashes of yellow rage.

'I won't come,' she said. 'Not this time.'

The eyes stayed on her. She felt a pressure in her feet, urging them to move. From the corridor came a sound of stumbling, then Mum's voice.

'Maya!'

She blundered out of the room to see Mum staggering towards her.

'Mum, what's happened?'

Mum stopped and leaned against her.

'I don't know,' she said. 'I've come over queasy too.'

'You look more than queasy. You look like Dad and Tommy.'

'Maya, listen.' Mum seized her by the arms. 'Are you all right?'

'I'm—'

'Answer me straight. Are you feeling ill? Weak, queasy, whatever?'

'No, I'm—'

'Stay here!' Mum tightened her grip. 'Do you hear? Don't leave The Rowan Tree under any circumstances. I've got to ring the emergency services. One doctor's not going to be enough. I don't know what's going on, but we need more help and we need it quick. I must check Milly's all right. And Roxy and Jake.'

'Mum—'

'Don't go outside The Rowan Tree!'

And Mum was gone. Maya stood there, staring after her. The growl came back. She whirled round and glared in the direction of her room.

'I know what you want,' she said, 'but I won't come.'

She started to walk down the corridor. The stairs appeared before her. She looked down them, then towards Tom's room. She should stay here. Tom needed her, Dad needed her, Mum needed her. She closed her eyes and saw flashes of yellow inside her brow.

'I won't come,' she muttered.

There was nothing she could do for Annie and Bryn. She knew that. The evil was here. It was attacking her family. She had to stay with them. She opened her eyes and saw yellow all around her. She ran down the stairs and through the drawing room to the side door. Mum's words rang in her head.

Don't go outside The Rowan Tree.

'I won't,' she said aloud, 'but I'm going to get rid of that bloody fox.'

She yanked open the door and stood there, scanning the path. The animal had jumped down from the garage roof and was now at the edge of the lawn, pawing the ground. She snarled at it.

'Go away!'

It went on pawing the ground, urging her with its eyes.

She stepped onto the path, picked up a stone. The animal stood there rigid, watching her.

'I'm staying,' she hissed. 'You understand? I'm staying with my family. I'm never coming with you again. So go away. And don't ever come back.'

The fox didn't move. It simply watched.

'Damn you!' she said.

She drew back her arm but before she could throw the stone, something caught her wrist from behind. She heard a grunt, felt a hood pulled over her head, a hand clapped over her mouth, then she was lifted off her feet and bundled away.

She writhed and struck out but it was no good. She was held in a grip too powerful to break. She tried to scream, but the hand over her mouth only tightened, the hood tightening with it.

It was a garden refuse bag. She could smell it. The kidnapper must have crept into the garden, stolen one of the bags from the shed, and waited by the side door. The fox had won again.

She tried again to scream. As before, the hand tightened over her mouth, and the tramping feet continued. She tried to think, to stay calm, but all she could do was struggle and squirm in a turbulence of black despair—and then she lay still. It was obvious she couldn't escape.

The steps went on, relentlessly. She'd given up all thoughts of resistance. She knew there was no point, and besides, she needed to save her strength. There might just be a chance to run later; and if she was to die tonight, she would need her strength to face that too. She closed her eyes and thought of Mum and Dad and Tom.

'I'm sorry,' she murmured.

Then suddenly the tramping stopped. She felt a jolt as she was half-placed, half-dropped on the ground. The bag

159

stayed over her head but the hands that had gripped her disappeared. She curled up, waiting. But nothing touched her.

Then she heard a moan.

It came again, close by. She sensed the kidnapper was standing over her. She thought of Zep. This didn't feel like him. She'd have expected mockery. She reached up, hesitantly, feeling for the bag over her head. She felt sure her hand would be stopped at any moment.

But nothing blocked it. She pulled the bag away and looked round. She was in a glade of trees, dusk closing in. There was no sign of the kidnapper. Then she heard the moan again, and this time a voice. It was coming from the other side of an oak tree.

'Bonny . . .'

She scrambled to her feet and moved to the right, keeping back from the oak. The lumbering form of Mo was bent over a figure slumped against the tree. The boy twisted his head to look at her and the word struggled out of his mouth again.

'Bonny . . .'

His hands were pounding his sides. He started to moan again, then suddenly strode towards Maya, his face dark, spittle round his mouth.

'Mo,' she said, 'don't hurt me.'

He grabbed her by the wrist and pulled.

'Mo, please.'

She lost her footing and slipped. He took no notice and simply dragged her over the ground towards the other side of the tree.

'Mo, you're hurting me.'

He let go.

'Bonny,' he mumbled.

The girl was slumped against the side of the tree, her

head drooping. Mo bent down, prodded Bonny's shoulder, shook it, then grabbed Maya by the wrist again.

'Mo, let go!' she said.

He thrust her hand towards Bonny and stabbed it against the girl's shoulder.

'Mo, let go of me.' She forced herself to look him in the face. 'I know what you want.'

The boy went on moaning and it was hard to tell whether he'd understood her or not. Then he let go. Maya edged closer to Bonny.

'Bonny, can you hear me?'

No answer came. She felt for a pulse, waited, waited.

And there it was—a flicker, but clear.

'Mo,' she said quickly, 'she's alive.'

But Mo was not there. She turned and searched the darkening glade. There was no sign of him and all was quiet. Then she caught a sound over to the left. She stared into the gloom and heard a wrenching of branches, a thrashing of leaves.

Then he reappeared, a giant shadow striding towards her. He'd found or torn off a heavy, club-like branch and he was brandishing it above his head. He broke into a run and charged at her.

'No!' she shouted.

She dived over Bonny's body, pulled it close, and braced herself for the blow. But it never came. Mo thundered past, roaring, and vanished into the forest behind them. The dusk closed over the place where he had been, and silence fell once more.

Then a voice broke it: a tired, barely-audible voice.

'You got to stop him.'

'Bonny!' said Maya.

She drew back and looked into the girl's face. Bonny's eyes were open, but only just.

'You got to stop him, Maya.'

'What's happened?'

Bonny took a slow breath.

'He knows who's behind this. He definitely knows.'

'Who is it?'

'No idea,' said Bonny. 'But whoever it is got me too. Don't ask me how.'

'My mum and dad are the same,' said Maya. 'And Tom.'

'Like me?'

'Yeah. I shouldn't be here, but Mo kidnapped me.'

Bonny watched, her mouth gaping with laboured breaths.

'I'm sorry,' she said eventually. 'He'd have . . . he'd have gone straight for you. Moment he found me like this.'

'Why me?' said Maya.

'Cos you're the only other person he'd ever trust,' said Bonny. 'I could see he was OK with you that time we walked you home. He's not like that with anybody else. He'd have looked for you straightaway. To try and make me right again.'

'But what happened to you?'

'Don't know,' said Bonny. 'We were meant to meet at the old barn, me and Mo. I told you before—it's one of the few places he can find by himself. I told him when to be there, then I went off to get some food for him. But he never turned up at the barn. It happens sometimes, even with places he knows. Something confuses him and then he panics and runs off and I have to go and find him.'

Bonny managed another breath.

'So I went looking for him in the forest,' she went on. 'No sign. Went back to the barn, waited for a bit, still no sign, so I went off looking again. And then I started feeling ill. Next thing I remember is Mo finding me here, and then I blacked out. Till now. Like I say, he'll have panicked and gone looking for you.'

Bonny stared at her.

'I'm sorry if he hurt you. He wouldn't have meant to.'

'I'm all right,' said Maya. 'But I'm scared, Bonny.'

'You got a mobile on you?'

'No.'

'Neither have I.' Bonny gulped in some more breaths. 'You're going to have to go and get help. Police, ambulance, anyone. And listen . . . you got to find Mo.'

'Bonny—'

'You got to find Mo. It's important, Maya. Cos someone's going to get murdered. Mo's looking to kill whoever's behind this. What's happened to me, I mean. He won't be thinking of anything else. Kill the person who killed me. That's what's in his head. But Maya, listen.'

Bonny's voice was growing softer.

'This person wants Mo dead too,' she said. 'Cos Mo knows too much. And he won't have a chance. He's strong and he's angry but he's not clever. You got to do something, Maya. You got to help Mo.'

Maya looked round the glade. The dusk was thickening and something grey was gliding through it. She watched. It was an owl; she could make it out now. But then it was gone.

'Bonny?' she said.

There was no answer.

'Oh, God.'

She felt for a pulse again. To her relief, it was still there, but the girl's eyes were closed and her head was drooping once more. Maya stared at her, willing the eyes to open, but they did not. She stood up.

Get help. Find Mo.

The words sounded in her head.

163

But she knew it was too late. There was only one choice left now and it had been made for her the day she first walked into the forest. She turned towards the spot where Mo had run off; and there among the darkening trees were the yellow eyes.

Beckoning.

She walked slowly towards them. They closed, then opened again, this time further off. She walked on towards them. She knew where they were leading her. The trees slipped by on either side. Even in the gathering dark she could see the headless images ripped from the bark.

She walked on past, following the yellow eyes, always just ahead, always in control. The picture of what awaited her was firm in her mind, and here it was already: the clearing, the damaged beech tree, though she'd come at it from a different angle.

She stared up at the cradle of ropes supporting the weakened branch; then gazed round. The yellow eyes were gone. Bryn's body was lying as she'd seen it before; so was Annie's, over in the thicket. She could see the horseshoe pendant glinting in the darkness, as bright and clear as Bryn's silver watch.

She thought of the other two figures she'd seen at the top of the clearing and stared in that direction. A dark form was sprawled there among the trees. But there was no figure standing over it. She glanced round.

Nobody.

She forced herself to walk past Bryn and Annie and on towards the body at the top of the clearing. It was hard to make much out in the darkness but she saw as she drew nearer that it was a large form. She crept closer.

The body lay motionless, still hard to see. She thought of the figure that wasn't there: the standing figure she'd seen before. It had craned over this body, and then sensed her. She looked nervously about her again, but she was still alone with whoever this was.

Then she recognized the face.

'Mo,' she murmured, bending over him.

He was breathing but he was badly hurt. His face and chest were sticky with blood. Even in the darkness she could see where a blade had slashed into his neck. The club-like branch he'd been carrying was nowhere to be seen.

'Darling Mo,' she whispered.

He opened his eyes, saw her, but didn't move. She sensed that he couldn't. Then his mouth twitched, as though he wanted to speak.

'What is it?' she said. 'Try and tell me.'

There was no answer. She leaned closer, her eyes on his. She was sure they were trying to say something. They whirled and swirled, carrying her mind with them, and then it came to her: the picture she'd seen before but in a new way.

The standing figure had been her. She'd seen herself that time, bending over Mo. But now the boy was starting to moan. She stared at him.

'What are you trying to tell me?'

He went on moaning, a loud, insistent sound. Her mind was racing. She thought of the picture again. Four figures: Annie, Bryn, Mo, herself. That was what she'd seen.

'Ah!' said Mo.

And then she understood.

There'd been a fifth person here that time, a figure she hadn't seen, because she'd been that person too: the witness of all this. She'd seen Annie and Bryn, seen Mo lying on the ground and her own image standing over him; then seen that image sense a presence behind it, and straighten, and turn.

She stared into Mo's eyes, and then straightened, and turned.

And saw a new figure standing there, on the very spot where she herself had looked on. The face was covered with a fox-mask, the body with fox-fur. The eyes radiated a predatory joy. The figure watched for a few moments, then drew a hand down the bark of the nearest tree.

Scratch, scratch, scratch.

Then reached behind the trunk.

And pulled out an axe.

23

'Leave us alone, Zep,' said Maya.

The fox-figure hissed, swayed, swung the axe from side to side: a heavy blade on a heavy shaft. Maya watched with dread. She knew what its real purpose was, what it had already done to Rebecca Flint. She heard a moan from Mo and looked quickly down at him. The boy's eyes were whirling as before.

'It's all right, Mo,' she murmured.

She stared at the fox-figure, now edging towards them.

'Go back, Zep!' she said.

Mo gave another moan but she kept her eyes on the fox-figure. She dared not glance away now. She braced herself. Fight was the only choice. She knew she couldn't desert Mo. The fox-figure raised the axe.

'No!' she shouted.

She stepped over Mo's body and tried to catch the shaft as it swung; but the movement was a feint. The blade scythed harmlessly past her and the butt of the handle whipped round and smashed into her cheek.

'Ah!'

She staggered back, pain ripping through her, but somehow stayed on her feet. The fox-figure ghosted right, swung the shaft towards her. She saw it coming but her parry was too late, and the butt rammed into her stomach.

She crumpled gasping over Mo, her head pounding from the first blow. She knew she had to act quickly, turn and face the figure and somehow block the blade, but her movements were laboured. She felt the figure draw near, saw the axe swing high.

She heard another hiss from the figure, caught a flashing downward movement, then a lunge from Mo as the boy thrust an arm past her. She squirmed round and looked up to see the fox-eyes glaring and Mo's hand clenched round the shaft.

But she knew it wouldn't last. Mo was too badly hurt and his grip was failing already. With a savage jerk the fox-figure wrenched the shaft clear, kicked Mo back to the ground, and raised the axe again. Maya closed her eyes.

She knew it was over, and that Mo knew it too. She could feel his body quivering against her. She heard a thud, then silence, and Mo was still. She squeezed herself into a ball, shaking. But there was no further blow. Only silence as before. She waited, still shaking, then slowly opened her eyes and looked round.

Mo was sprawled out in the darkness.

So too was the fox-figure.

Zep was standing over it.

He was not in fox-disguise. He was in rough clothes and he was holding Mo's improvised club. The fox-figure lay face down at his feet, twitching. Zep stared at it, then with a sudden roar he lifted the club and brought it hard down. The body twitched once more and was still. Zep growled at it, then dropped the club and seized the axe.

'No!' Maya jumped to her feet. 'Zep, don't!'

He glared at her, the axe high.

'What do you care, townie?'

'Don't do it, Zep.'

'Why not?'

'Just don't.'

Zep stood there, glowering.

'Please, Zep.'

She took a step closer to him, trying to ignore the pain, and her terror of this boy.

'You've got to get help,' she said. 'Mo's badly hurt. And something terrible's happened to my mum and dad, and Tom, and Bonny, and Bryn and Annie down there in the clearing. They could all be dead. Like Rebecca Flint.'

'Yeah,' Zep muttered. 'Like Rebecca Flint.'

He spat on the fox-figure lying at his feet.

'And I'm hurt too,' she said.

He looked up at her, his eyes still raging.

'Put the axe down, Zep. Please.'

He went on scowling at her, then whirled round and with an anguished yell flung the axe into the trees. Maya crouched over Mo again. The boy was flat on his back but he was still breathing. She took his hand and saw his eyes open.

'I thought you were dead,' she murmured. 'I heard a thud and thought it was you getting killed. But it was Zep knocking the fox-figure off us. He saved us. You're going to be OK.'

Mo started whimpering. She squeezed his hand.

'Bonny's thinking of you,' she whispered. 'She's thinking of you right now.'

Out of the corner of her eye she saw Zep watching her. She glanced round at him.

'You've got to get help, Zep,' she said.

He stared back, clenching and unclenching his hands.

'Have you got a mobile?' she said.

He didn't answer.

'Zep,' she said, 'you've got to do something. If you've got a mobile, ring for help. Or give me the mobile and I'll ring. Or run down to the clearing and check Bryn and Annie. One of them'll have a phone. Bring it back here.'

Zep didn't move.

'Zep,' she said, 'there might be time to save people.'

Still Zep didn't move. She let go of Mo's hand and stood up.

'Zep, do it!'

But Zep turned away and ran off into the trees.

'Zep!' she called after him.

All she heard was the pounding of his feet as he put on speed, then all was still again, save for Mo's soft weeping. She knelt beside him and took his hand again. He fixed his strange eyes upon her.

'Mo, listen,' she said. 'I'm going down to the clearing, OK? I've got to find a mobile. There's two people down there. One of them might have a phone.'

'Bonny,' murmured the boy.

'I know,' she said. 'You want to see her so much.'

His hand was squeezing hers now and she could feel his fear, his desperate loneliness.

'It's all right, Mo,' she said. 'I promise I'll come straight back.'

'Bonny,' he muttered.

'I'll come straight back.'

She eased her hand from his and stood up again. Mo gave a moan, flapped his arms, made as if to stand up, then sank back. The blood was flowing more freely from his neck. She took a long breath. Her own pain was growing worse and she knew she had to move now.

She broke away, ignoring Mo's sobs, and stumbled across the clearing. Bryn's body was closer. She knelt down and looked into his face. There was no sign of life in it.

'Bryn,' she said, 'can you hear me?'

No answer. Mo's sobs were growing louder and he was now bellowing Bonny's name into the night. She made herself focus on Bryn. No movement in the stomach or

170

chest as far as she could see, though it was hard to make much out in the darkness. She took his wrist, felt for a pulse, waited.

And there it was: a low, fluttering beat.

But how much time he had she couldn't tell. She fumbled through his pockets. There had to be a mobile. He must surely have one. Here it was. She clutched it and stood up, swaying. Mo was now screaming Bonny's name.

'I'm coming, Mo!' she called. 'I'm coming!'

But she had to check Annie first. She lurched over to the policewoman and knelt down. No pulse. Nothing at all.

'Come on, Annie,' she said. 'Please.'

Then she felt it, just like Bryn's: a low, reluctant beat. Or perhaps a defiant one.

'Annie, can you hear me?'

No answer. She searched through the pockets, found a mobile and with an effort stood up again. Mo's screams were now louder than ever.

'I'm coming, Mo!' she called.

But she was struggling to move now. She could feel consciousness going, balance going. Somehow she reached the trees at the top of the clearing. But to her horror, Mo had vanished—and his screams had stopped.

Then she saw him. He'd dragged himself over to the left and slumped against a tree. She tottered over to him and knelt down. He was still muttering Bonny's name and his eyes were throwing fiery glances at her, and past her shoulder.

'I know,' she said. 'You're angry with me for leaving you. And you're frightened of the fox-figure.'

She looked round at the unmoving form, still face down with the fur and mask in place. She had no wish to go closer. She rested a hand on Mo's shoulder.

'I'll take care of you,' she said. 'I promise I will.'

She checked the phones and frowned. Both were switched off. She'd been hoping at least one of them would be on. But it might still work. She switched on Bryn's and waited.

'Don't ask me for a security code,' she murmured. 'Please, please, please.'

It did.

'Damn.'

She tried Annie's phone. But it was the same.

She looked at Mo. He was watching her with deep attention, his eyes wide. She sensed a trust in them, but she knew that was about to be lost. Because now she had to leave him. There was no other way to get help.

'I'm sorry, Mo,' she said.

Then she saw something.

Beyond the boy's shoulder, in the deeper folds of the forest.

Two yellow dots, bright against the darkness.

She watched, breathing hard. Something touched her arm, something large and heavy. She knew it was Mo's hand. She took it in her own but kept her eyes on the yellow dots. The hand gripped hers, squeezed tight. She looked round.

'It's all right, Mo,' she said. 'I'm not going to leave you.'

The blood was now pouring from his neck. The boy's mouth moved and Bonny's name slipped from it. Maya reached out with her other hand and touched his face.

'Please don't die,' she whispered.

She looked back at the two dots. They were brighter now as they watched from the trees; and as she watched them back, she heard the growl of the fox, low but clear. The yellow eyes closed, opened, closed again; and in the space where they had been, she saw torches drawing near.

24

The Rowan Tree. Maya lay back in the armchair, Doctor Wade and the nurse checking her head-bandage. Milly, Jake, and Roxy sat round, watching. From upstairs came the sound of footsteps. Maya looked up.

'Keep still, love,' said the nurse.

'Nearly done,' said Doctor Wade.

Maya said nothing. She was glad Doctor Wade had been sent out to join the paramedics. But nothing mattered if Mum or Dad or Tom were dead. She winced as the nurse tightened the bandage.

'Easy, Maya,' said the nurse.

'How's the pain now?' asked Doctor Wade.

'Still throbbing,' said Maya, 'but it's gone down a bit.'

'Give it time. The medication takes a while to kick in.'

'The main thing is,' said the nurse, 'that you're still with us. And this will heal. You're not going to look your best for a week or two, but it'll clear up and you'll be fine.'

Maya thought back to the forest: the glare of torches, the rush of police and paramedics. It felt like a blur to her now, too many images to make sense of. All she remembered was crowds: round Mo, round Annie, round Bryn, round the fox-figure—and a crowd round herself, checking her over, asking questions, then carrying her off through the trees. She had no idea what had happened to the others.

'All finished, Maya,' said the nurse.

Jake leaned forward.

'I'm making you another hot chocolate,' he said. 'You didn't touch the last one and it's gone cold.'

But before he could leave the room, the door opened and DI Henderson walked in. Maya closed her eyes. If it was going to be bad news, she didn't want to look at him, or anyone. She heard his footsteps draw near.

'They're going to be OK,' he said.

She looked up at him. He drew a chair close and sat down.

'It was a home-made poison,' he said. 'Or maybe I should call it a nature-made poison, since most of the ingredients seem to have come from the forest, or wild places at least. A lethal mixture and amateur in the sense that you wouldn't be able to buy it anywhere, but certainly not amateur in the way it was put together.'

'Tell me about Mum and Dad,' said Maya. 'And Tom.'

'They're all right,' said the officer. 'Sleeping soundly and they probably won't wake till tomorrow. Doctor Kahn reckons everything's under control now, but she says recovery's going to take some time, OK? Your mum and dad and brother aren't going to have much energy at first, and there may be more bouts of queasiness and even vomiting. But the worst's over, she says, so I think you can relax a bit now.'

Maya looked down, fighting tears.

'You're going to feel very shaken up too, Maya,' said Doctor Wade, 'and for quite a while. If I were you, I'd take up Jake's offer of a hot chocolate, drink it this time, and then get to bed. You know they're all sleeping now, and if you could just get some rest yourself, then hopefully you'll all wake up feeling better and ready to talk properly in the morning.'

Maya shook her head. She couldn't rest yet. She knew that.

'Mo,' she muttered, 'and Annie and Bryn and . . . '

'Rest first, Maya,' said Milly. 'Rest first, eh?'

'No.' She looked at DI Henderson. 'Tell me. Even if it's bad.'

The officer frowned.

'Annie and Bryn have been taken to the hospital in Cresswell,' he said. 'I'm told things are looking promising. The paramedics only just got to them in time, but fortunately Doctor Kahn's team had already started treating your parents and Tom here, and they'd also had a chance to examine the poison with some of our specialists, so they were able to pass useful information on to the operatives in the forest.'

'But how did you know where to send them?' said Maya.

'Educated guess,' said the policeman. 'When Milly told us you'd disappeared again, it seemed likely you might end up by the old beech tree. Since you'd mentioned that place before. Bit of a hunch but I'm glad we were right.'

'I'm making that hot chocolate now,' said Jake, and he was gone.

Maya looked at DI Henderson again.

'I know,' he said. 'You want me to tell you about Mo and Bonny.'

'Yes.'

'Mo's not good at all,' he said. 'Touch and go, I'm afraid. He got badly slashed in the neck and he's lost a lot of blood. Can't say any more for now. Except that he's in intensive care at the same hospital as the others. As for Bonny . . . we haven't been able to find her.'

Maya burst into tears.

'It's my fault,' she said.

'No, it's not,' said the officer.

'It is.' She wiped her eyes and stared at him. 'One of the

policemen . . . in the forest . . . I told him about Bonny and he asked me where she was.'

'Exactly,' said DI Henderson. 'You did your best to help.'

'But I didn't help,' she said. 'I tried to remember where she was but I got confused on my way to the clearing and I didn't know where I was going, and I knew I wasn't making sense to the policeman, and then the ambulance people were carrying me off, and now I've left Bonny to die and—'

'No, you haven't,' said Milly.

'Milly's right,' said DI Henderson. 'You did very well with the officer in the forest. And I can promise you our people have searched all round the area where you were. If Bonny was anywhere there, they'd have found her.'

'But she couldn't move,' said Maya.

'It still doesn't mean she's dead,' said the policeman. 'You know how stubborn Bonny is. She probably came round and struggled off somewhere by sheer will power. We don't even know what caused her to collapse. It seems unlikely she was poisoned like the others.'

'She's probably lying dead somewhere,' said Maya. 'And it's my fault.'

She saw Roxy crying too.

'I'm sorry, Roxy,' she said.

Roxy looked up.

'It wasn't your fault, Maya.'

'Was Bonny your friend?'

Roxy shook her head.

'I didn't like her. And she didn't like me. But I never wanted her dead.'

'No one's saying she's dead,' said Doctor Wade.

Maya felt weariness flooding through her. She yearned to sleep now but there was still so much she had to know. Jake reappeared with a new mug of hot chocolate.

'I'm going to stand here and watch you drink it,' he said.

She took the mug from him, blew on the hot chocolate, and sipped.

'Good?' said Jake.

She looked up at him. His face seemed strange, as though it was being pulled by different impulses. She could tell that he had one very clear set of feelings towards her; but he was trying to be brotherly too and it made him seem awkward, though in a touching way.

'It's good,' she said. 'Thanks.'

Jake glanced at Roxy.

'You've been crying,' he said.

'Mo's in intensive care,' she said, 'and Bonny's still missing.'

'Oh, Christ,' he said.

The nurse stirred.

'I must be getting back upstairs.'

'I'll come with you,' said Doctor Wade.

She looked at Maya.

'You really need to sleep, Maya. Milly'll look after you. Milly, you're staying the night, aren't you?'

'I'm staying for however long it takes,' said Milly.

'That might be some days,' said Doctor Wade. 'Mr and Mrs Munro won't be active for a while. Nor will Tom.'

'Can I go up and see them now?' said Maya.

'I'll check with Doctor Kahn,' said the nurse. 'If I'm not down again in two minutes, you can look in on your way to bed. But remember, they'll be sleeping.'

And she and Doctor Wade left the room.

DI Henderson's mobile rang.

'Excuse me,' he said, and he took the phone outside.

Maya turned to Milly.

'I know what you're wondering,' said Milly.

'How did they get poisoned?'

'It was in the beef casserole.'

'Who put it there?' said Maya.

'Don't know.'

Maya stared at her.

'Haven't the police found out who the fox-figure is?' she said.

'If they have,' said Jake, 'they haven't told us.'

'They're keeping their cards close,' said Milly. 'No doubt we'll get told things when we're allowed to hear 'em.'

Maya finished the hot chocolate and put the mug down.

'So how come you three didn't get poisoned?'

'We never had none of the casserole,' said Milly, 'nor did your mum and dad, or Tom. So whatever they had earlier, there must have been poison in that too. You didn't eat nothing most of the day, so you was all right, and Jake and Roxy and me ate separate, so we was OK. Bryn and Annie chose the casserole from the menu and that's how they got caught.'

'But how did the poison get in the casserole?' said Jake.

'Good question,' said Milly.

Maya frowned, aware of an answer growing in her mind, though it didn't seem possible. She thought of the scratching sound: on the doors here, on the tree by the edge of the clearing—and the axe swinging in the dark.

DI Henderson came back in.

'They've found Bonny,' he said. 'Seems she came to again after Maya left her and managed to stagger to Jim Tozer's farm. One of Jim's sons found her collapsed outside the door and called the emergency services. They're out there now.'

'Is she going to be OK?' said Roxy.

'Too early to say,' said the officer, 'but it looks like she got poisoned too.'

'But how?' said Jake.

'Turns out,' said DI Henderson, 'from what Bonny's just told the officer there that she and Mo have been hanging round one of the barns on Griff Gordon's land. She says she went to meet Mo there, found he hadn't turned up, so she left some food for him in case he showed, and then went looking for him. Came back, still no sign, but she ate some of the stuff she'd left for him and then went off again, and collapsed. So either the poison was in the food already or—more likely—it got added to it while it was sitting in the barn and Bonny was off looking for Mo.'

'So that means,' said Milly, 'that the person who did this knew Bonny and Mo were meeting at the barn. And followed Bonny there in secret.'

'Exactly,' said the policeman. 'Either to kill her or kill him. Or both.'

His eyes flickered towards Maya.

'I knew they met there,' she said.

'I thought you might.'

'I saw them there,' she said. 'That time I got chased by Zep.'

'Go on.'

'I ended up at the barn by chance. Zep came up and threatened me. But then Mo appeared and Zep backed off. And Bonny turned up. I promised her I wouldn't tell anyone they met there. Because Bonny said Mo knew who was behind all the trouble. She was frightened for him.'

'So Zep knew they were meeting there too?'

'Yes,' she said. 'Well, he saw Mo there anyway.'

'I see.'

'I'm sorry I didn't tell you the truth before.'

DI Henderson studied her for a moment, then went on. 'There's one other thing I can tell you,' he said. 'We've done some more tests, in the light of what's happened today, and it seems Rebecca Flint was poisoned too.'

'But hang on,' said Jake. 'I thought she was—'

'Yes, I know,' said DI Henderson. 'She was . . . mutilated . . . and it's highly probable that the axe we found in the forest tonight was the weapon used. But she was poisoned first.'

He paused.

'The same concoction, hard to detect by taste, slow acting to give no immediate warning, and designed to disable over a period of hours. Mrs Flint would have lost her strength, just as Mr and Mrs Munro did, and the others, and when she was dead, or too weak to resist, she was mutilated and buried outside The Rowan Tree.'

'But why have all these things happened?' said Milly.

'That's something we still don't know,' said the officer.

Maya thought of the effigy under the floorboard, the figures carved into the trees—and then Mo's face, peering up at her with his strange eyes.

'Have you found Zep?' she murmured.

'Not yet,' said DI Henderson. 'But we're looking hard.'

'And what about—'

'No,' said the officer.

She looked sharply at him. He shook his head.

'I can't tell you about the fox-figure. I know you want me to.'

'We all do,' said Milly.

'I appreciate that,' said DI Henderson. 'But I'm not in a position yet to make any kind of statement about this person.'

He looked back at Maya.

'We're obviously going to need to talk again,' he said. 'But right now I suggest you get some sleep. I'll look in again tomorrow.'

'Thanks for your help,' said Milly.

'No problem,' said the officer. 'Good night to you all.'

And DI Henderson took his leave.

Maya felt her bandage. The pain was easing slightly but exhaustion was overwhelming her. Milly touched her on the arm.

'Come on,' she said. 'You're dropping. Roxy and Jake got to get home too. But I'll be here all night, OK? I'll be sleeping in the room next to you, so I won't be far away.'

'Thanks, Milly,' said Maya. 'But . . . '

She hesitated.

'But what?' said Milly.

Maya stood up and looked at Jake.

'I want you to help me find something,' she said.

25

Mum, Dad, and Tom were in adjacent rooms. Doctor Kahn stood with Maya in each of the doorways and they looked in together. All three were sleeping soundly.

'It's lucky we were called out so promptly,' said Doctor Kahn. 'It meant we were able to take corrective action before the thing really got hold. But listen . . .'

She looked closely at Maya.

'The healing process is going to take time, OK? Your mum and dad and Tom are going to be weak for quite a while and they may suffer bouts of nausea and possibly more vomiting.'

'But they're not in danger, are they?' said Maya.

'Not any more,' said Doctor Kahn. 'We wouldn't be letting them stay here if we weren't sure of that. We'd have them in hospital with Annie and Bryn.'

'Are Annie and Bryn going to be all right?'

'We hope so,' said Doctor Kahn. 'They're making progress, but they took more of the poison than your parents and Tom did, and they were also lying untreated for a longer period. So it's a bit more complicated with them.'

'What about Bonny?'

'I don't have any information on her. Or the boy with the neck wound.'

Maya heard a sound behind her and turned. Jake was standing there, flanked by Roxy and Milly.

'It's time everyone got some rest,' said Doctor Kahn.

'Maya's the one who's got to rest,' said Milly.

'That's certainly true.' Doctor Kahn looked at Maya. 'There's nothing more you can do here for now. Nothing more any of us can do. My colleagues and I are just leaving too.'

'But isn't that risky?' said Maya.

'Not at all,' said Doctor Kahn. 'Don't worry. Milly knows exactly what to do and she's got an emergency number to call if anything happens. But I don't think there'll be a problem. Your parents and Tom should sleep through the night and hopefully well into the morning. And Doctor Wade'll be back first thing to check all's well.'

Doctor Wade and the nurse joined her.

'Thanks for all your help,' said Milly.

'Thanks,' said Maya.

'No problem at all,' said Doctor Kahn.

'I'll come down with you,' said Milly.

Maya watched them go, then turned to Jake and Roxy.

'What did you want me to help you find?' said Jake.

'You're probably too tired now,' she said.

'Not as tired as you are,' said Jake. 'You ought to be sleeping. Can't it wait till the morning?'

'No, I . . . ' She resisted the urge to lean against the wall. 'I want to do this now. I must. It's important.'

'OK,' said Jake.

From downstairs came the sound of the front door opening and closing, then footsteps outside, and then Milly's returning to the foot of the stairs.

'Maya,' she called.

Maya walked to the top of the stairs. Milly was standing at the bottom, looking up.

'Bed, Maya,' she said. 'Jake and Roxy got to call it a day too. They're out on their feet. Whatever Jake says.'

'Five minutes,' said Maya.

She felt Jake and Roxy appear behind her. Milly stared up at them all, then nodded.

'Five minutes,' she said. 'No more.'

And she disappeared down the corridor.

'Tell us what you want,' said Jake.

'We want to help,' said Roxy.

Maya looked from one to the other.

'The person who did all this,' she began.

'The fox-figure?' said Roxy.

'Yes,' said Maya. 'He had an obsession. I know he did.'

'With what?' said Jake.

'The Rowan Tree.'

She glanced round her.

'He was haunting this place.'

'You mean he was actually here?' said Roxy.

'Yes.'

'Inside The Rowan Tree?'

'Yes,' said Maya. 'I heard him. He was trying to frighten me. And he did. I heard scratching on the bedroom door. Nobody believed me but I heard it. And when I was in the forest, the fox-figure reached out and made the same scratching noise on a tree.'

'That's horrible,' said Roxy.

'And I found something . . . ' Maya pictured it. 'Under the floorboards in my room. I didn't tell anyone about it. But . . . I found a kind of . . . effigy. Like those headless bodies carved into the trees. I threw it away in the forest. I just know the fox-figure's been inside The Rowan Tree. And he put the poison in the food.'

'But why?' said Roxy. 'Why did he do all this?'

'I don't know,' said Maya. 'But I want to find out where he got in. And where he hid. Can you help me? I just . . . won't rest till I know.'

'Come on,' said Jake.

And he strode off down the corridor in the direction of her room.

'Where are you going?' said Maya.

'Come on,' he called back.

Roxy set off after him, and after a moment Maya too, though she could feel fear rising again. She had no intention of going in her room. She was still too frightened of it. But Jake seemed determined to take her there. Then he stopped, just before it.

'What is it?' said Roxy. 'Something in Maya's room?'

Jake shook his head.

'Here,' he said, and he nodded towards the broom cupboard.

'There's a secret compartment in there. I told Tom about it. It's not that interesting. But it's bigger than the one in the attic room. Worth a look anyway.'

He pulled open the door and switched on the light.

Maya peered in. It was a musty little space and she'd never looked closely at it before. Nor, apparently, had Mum and Dad since they clearly hadn't found a proper use for it. There were a couple of brooms in there, and a mop, and an old vacuum cleaner, but it was mostly a dumping ground for towels and sheets that didn't fit in the airing cupboard.

'Not much of a hiding place,' she said.

'Now look,' said Jake.

And he felt round the panelling to the right. At first nothing seemed to happen, then she heard a click, and now the panel board was sliding across as Jake eased it with his hands. Behind it was another space, the same size as the broom cupboard.

And empty.

Save for one thing.

The trace in the air of a hostile presence.

'There's nothing in there,' said Roxy.

'Maybe I was wrong,' said Jake. 'I just thought it seemed the obvious place to hide.'

'He used it,' said Maya.

They looked round at her.

'He used it,' she said. 'I know he did.'

'How can you be so sure?' said Roxy. 'It's just an empty space. There's no clue to suggest he hid in here. And even if he did, it doesn't explain how he got into The Rowan Tree in the first place. I mean, I know there's the downstairs doors and maybe the windows, if one of them was open, but it's hard to know how he could have used them without someone seeing him.'

'He didn't use the doors,' said Jake. 'Or the windows.'

He was staring at something in the far corner. To Maya, it was hidden in shadow and she was too far back to see clearly, but now Jake was kneeling down to look more closely. She and Roxy squeezed together and peered over his shoulder.

He was bent over the floorboards.

'These are loose,' he said. 'They never used to be. I mean, it's ages since I came in here but they used to be nice and snug and they were nailed down. But the nails have been taken out and the boards are just resting here.'

He started working away at the edges.

'Right,' he said. 'Now let's see.'

And he started to prise up the furthest floorboard. Maya felt Roxy take her hand. She looked round at her and smiled, and they went on watching together. Jake had now pulled the floorboard clear and was easing it up to vertical. The light from the broom cupboard behind them threw a slanted glow over the gap that had been revealed, but not enough to show more than the side of a heavy joist. Jake propped the floorboard against the panelling,

186

then bent down and peered through the opening.

'Can you see anything?' said Roxy.

'Not much,' he said. 'I could do with a torch. Is there one handy?'

Maya thought of the torch in her room. But she said nothing.

'I've got one in my rucksack,' said Roxy. 'I always carry one round the village.'

'You're better organized than I am,' said Jake.

'I'll get it,' said Roxy, and she was gone.

Jake was still peering through the gap; then suddenly he looked up.

'What is it?' said Maya.

'I know what's down there,' he said.

'You do?'

'Yeah. I don't need the torch to tell me.'

'Then why did you ask if—'

'I want you and Roxy to see it,' he said. 'And you'll need a torch for that.'

Maya stared at the gap.

'Have you . . . seen under these floorboards before?'

'No,' said Jake. 'But I guessed what's there. Moment I looked through the gap I knew I was right. I know how the fox-figure got in now. And where he stayed while he was here.'

'He stayed in my room,' she said.

He looked at her.

'Are you serious?'

'Yes,' she said.

'But not while you were there?'

'No,' she said. 'But when I wasn't there, he stayed in my room.'

'You're thinking of the effigy he left under the floorboard.'

'It's not just that.'

'What, then?' said Jake.

'I just . . . know he spent time in my room,' she said. 'He slept in there. During those months when The Rowan Tree was empty, before we moved in. I just . . . feel it. That's one reason why I'm scared of going in my room.'

Jake looked back at the gap in the floor.

'Well, he had other places at The Rowan Tree too.'

There was a sound of footsteps. Maya turned and saw Roxy back again, with Milly looking gruff.

'Maya,' she said, 'this is turning into a long five minutes.'

'I'm sorry, Milly,' said Maya, 'but it's really important.'

'Yes, yes,' said Milly, 'I've no doubt it is. Roxy says you're wanting a torch. Try this one. It's more powerful than the dinky thing she carries in her rucksack.'

Maya took the torch.

'Thanks, Milly.'

She held it out to Jake, but he shook his head.

'You look,' he said. 'And Roxy.'

He stood aside and let Maya and Roxy edge past.

'Best to kneel,' he said.

Maya knelt by the gap, aware that she was squeezing the torch very tight. She shone the beam onto the joist—and gave a start.

'Oh, God,' she murmured.

There was a headless figure.

Drawn in the dust.

She looked round at the others.

'I can see it,' said Jake.

'Nasty,' said Milly, peering over Roxy's shoulder.

'Look further,' said Jake. 'Look right into the gap.'

Maya bent closer and shone the beam through. Below her was a square, walled shaft descending into the darkness. The brick looked old and rough.

'It's an old chimney breast,' said Jake. 'I knew there was one but I didn't know it led up to this spot. It obviously doesn't go any further. The chimney's been disused all the years I've been at The Rowan Tree. But the brick looks pretty firm. And easy to climb.'

'Climb?' said Maya.

'Yes,' said Jake. 'He climbed up inside the chimney breast and waited in the secret compartment till it was safe to creep round the hotel.'

Maya pictured the fox-face emerging from the darkness below.

And shuddered.

'But where does the chimney breast start?' she said.

'In the cellar,' said Jake.

She straightened up and looked round at him.

'But there isn't a chimney in the cellar.'

She thought of the musty room at the bottom of The Rowan Tree. Mum and Dad used it to store wine, spirits, and beer. She'd been in there a few times but she'd never seen anything remotely like a chimney; and there was another problem with this theory.

'There's no outside door to the cellar,' she said. 'The only door's the one with the steps up to the kitchen. So the fox-figure couldn't have got into the cellar without going through the hotel first.'

'Yes, he could,' said Jake.

He reached out a hand to her. She took it and let him pull her up.

'I'll show you,' he said.

26

The moment they entered the cellar, she knew Jake was right. The hostile presence had been here too; she could feel it. Milly switched on the light.

'Let's cheer the place up a bit,' she said.

Roxy looked round.

'It's a bit scary down here.'

'Nothing to be scared of,' said Milly. 'You didn't use to be scared coming in here, did you?'

'No, but—'

'Whoever done this bad stuff is gone,' said Milly, 'and he ain't coming back. So there's nothing to be scared of now. Not in the cellar, nor nowhere at The Rowan Tree.'

'Still feels creepy,' said Roxy.

Maya too was looking round. There was still no sign of a chimney but she saw what Jake meant about a way in from the outside: something she'd barely noticed before.

The window high up the wall in the far corner: the only window here and just above ground level. It looked out onto the path round the east wing of the hotel. She stared at it, aware of Jake's eyes on her face.

'Did he get in there?' she said.

'I reckon,' said Jake.

He stepped over to the far corner, climbed on one of the beer barrels, and pushed the glass. The window opened easily and a draught of cool air whispered in.

'Catch is broken,' he said. 'Or it's been broken, more like.'

He studied it for a moment.

'Yeah,' he said, 'I'm pretty sure it's been messed with. Window shuts but not properly. Doesn't click. If you came from the other side, you could just pull it open and climb through. That's how he got in.'

'But there's still no chimney,' said Maya.

Jake jumped back off the barrel and walked up to her.

'Look over there,' he said.

And he nodded towards the far wall.

Maya stared at it.

'But it's just a wall,' she said.

Jake took her by the hand and walked her towards it, past rows of bottles and more beer barrels, Roxy and Milly following quietly.

'Here.' Jake stopped. 'See it now?'

'Just a wall,' said Maya.

He let go of her hand, eased a couple of heavy barrels to the side, and there it was: the clear shape of an old fireplace, now boarded over.

'I never saw that,' she said. 'I never ever saw that.'

'Why should you?' said Milly. 'You've only been at The Rowan Tree a few days. You've probably hardly ever been down here. And if you did, I don't suppose you came down this end. Why would you? And even then, the fireplace is hard to see with all those barrels and things in the way.'

Jake looked round at Maya.

'I'll bet you anything you want that board's not attached,' he said. 'It used to be. Let's see if it still is.'

He bent down and examined it.

'Told you,' he said. 'Same as the floorboards in the secret compartment. Nails have been taken out. But you

191

wouldn't notice unless you looked close.'

He felt round the edges and it didn't take long to work the board free.

'Stand back,' he said. 'It's heavier than it looks.'

And he eased it to one side.

'There you go,' he said.

But Maya turned away. Suddenly she'd seen enough and all she wanted was to run upstairs and be with Mum and Dad and Tom again. No one called after her. She stopped at the bottom of the steps to the kitchen and looked back at them.

They were still standing by the fireplace.

'Thank you,' she said.

She hurried back to the ground floor, along the corridor to the stairs, up to the first floor, and in to Mum's room, then Dad's, then Tom's. All were sleeping, as soundly as before. She heard the front door close and a few minutes later Milly reappeared.

'I sent Jake and Roxy off home,' she said. 'They wanted to stay longer, case there was anything they could do. I said no. Had to be firm or they'd still be here. They'll be back first thing in the morning. Now listen, young lady.'

She took both Maya's hands.

'I know what's going to happen if I don't make you. You'll stay up all night looking over these three. And it'll do no good, because they're going to sleep fine, whether you're watching them or not. So, listen. I've found your night clothes and your toothbrush and things, and I've made up a bed for you in Room Nine.'

Maya said nothing.

'You couldn't be closer to your mum and dad and Tom,' said Milly. 'Closer than your own bedroom. And anyway, you're not too keen on going in there right now, are you?'

'How come you—'

192

'Never mind how I know.' Milly took her by the arm. 'So I'm taking you to Room Nine now and I'm going to leave you in there for a couple of minutes, and then I'll look in again, and I'll be expecting you to be in bed with the light off, OK? I'm sleeping in Room Eight, so we're all near one another. Come on.'

Maya didn't want to move. She wanted to stay here, near the others. But she had no energy to resist. She let Milly take her to Room Nine, open the door, push her gently in, close the door. She undressed, put on her nightie, climbed into bed, turned off the light. She heard the door open, saw Milly's shadowy face look round, heard the door close again.

The light went off outside the room.

She closed her eyes, and sleep of a sort did come, but she soon woke again. The room was dark and her head was pounding, though the pain had lessened. She lay there, her thoughts on one thing alone.

She climbed out of bed, pulled on her dressing gown and slipped out of the room. No light was on in the corridor but as she made her way down it, she saw a dark shape that had not been there before. She stopped and stared, then saw what it was.

Milly, dozing in a chair.

She walked closer. She recognized the chair now. Milly had taken it from Room Six. She'd obviously decided not to sleep in a bed after all. Maya crept nearer, anxious not to wake her. The doors to Mum's room and Dad's were half-open and Milly had positioned her chair so that she could keep a check on both.

Maya looked into the first room.

Mum was still sleeping in exactly the same position as before; so too was Dad. She moved on to Tom's room. He was the same. She watched him for a few moments, then tiptoed into his room, took a cushion from the chair, and curled up on the floor at the foot of the bed, and fell asleep.

Some time later a voice woke her.

She opened her eyes and saw light seeping through the window. She twisted round on the floor. It felt hard beneath her and she had a crick in her neck. The voice spoke again.

'Sis?'

She stood up and walked round the bed. Tom was lying on his side, facing the window, his eyes still closed. He was breathing quietly, but steadily. She watched him for several minutes but he didn't speak again. Then he stirred, just a little, easing his body closer to the edge of the bed. She bent down and settled the duvet around him.

His eyes stayed closed, his body still. She went on watching him, aware of the dawn breaking, and the sound of snores from the corridor. She listened for a few moments, still watching Tom's face, then she bunched the duvet closer around him, returned to the foot of the bed, and lay down again on the floor.

Sleep rushed over her and she fell into it.

The next time she woke, sunlight was bright upon the window; and a new voice was speaking to her.

'Maya?'

She looked up and saw Dad standing over her.

'Maya,' he said.

She scrambled up off the floor and threw her arms round him.

'Careful,' he whispered. 'I'm a little fragile.'

'Are you OK?' she said.

'I'm going to be fine. We're all going to be fine.'

'Is Mum—'

'Still sleeping,' he said. 'And I'm meant to be sleeping

194

too. Or lying down anyway. Doctor Wade said I shouldn't be walking yet.'

'Is she here already?'

'Already?' Dad chuckled. 'Do you know what time it is?'

'No.'

'Eleven o'clock,' he said. 'The place is buzzing. We've got Doctor Wade here, Milly, Jake, Roxy, and DI Henderson. He's been here for ages, Milly says. Turned up first thing. I gather he wants a word with you, but she wouldn't let anyone wake you. So he's been sitting downstairs waiting.'

'Am I in trouble?'

'Don't be silly.'

Tom gave a moan, turned over and opened his eyes. Dad and Maya leaned over him together. He gave another moan, then yawned.

'Sis?' he said. 'Were you here while I was sleeping?'

'Yeah.'

'I didn't snore, did I?'

'No,' she said.

But Tom had already fallen asleep again. Dad tidied the duvet around him, then straightened up, swaying slightly.

'Are you OK?' said Maya.

'I'm not as steady as I thought I was,' he said. 'Doctor Wade did warn me. Can you give me a hand?'

She locked an arm round his and helped him out of the room. He was walking slowly, his face set. Doctor Wade was standing in the corridor, watching them approach.

'How are you, Maya?' she said.

'I'm OK.'

'How's the head?'

'Still hurting. But it's a bit better.'

'I'll take a look at that bandage later. Why don't you go in and say hello to your mum?'

'Has Mum woken up?' said Maya.

'Just this second.'

Mum was sitting up in bed, rubbing her eyes.

'Mum,' said Maya.

Mum held out her arms and Maya ran forward.

'Gently, Maya,' said Doctor Wade.

'It's OK,' said Mum.

Maya tumbled into her and they held each other for a few moments; then Mum eased her back and looked into her face.

'You all right?' she said.

'Yes, Mum.'

Mum went on studying her face.

'I'm all right, Mum,' said Maya. 'Really.'

'OK.' Mum glanced up at the others. 'Is that DI Henderson's voice I can hear downstairs?'

'Yes,' said Doctor Wade. 'He wants to speak to Maya.'

'I'd better go down and see him,' said Maya. She looked at Mum. 'Will you all be OK here?'

'We're fine,' said Mum. 'Stop worrying about us.'

Maya slipped back to Room Nine, washed and dressed as quickly as she could, and hurried downstairs. DI Henderson was sitting at the kitchen table, drinking coffee with Milly, Jake, and Roxy.

'What's the news?' she said.

The policeman looked up at her gravely, then stood up.

'Are your parents awake?' he said.

'Yes,' she said, 'but what's the news?'

'Excuse me.'

And he left the room without another word.

Maya sat down and looked at Milly.

'What's going on?' she said.

'No idea,' said Milly. 'He wouldn't tell us nothing. You better start your breakfast. There's coffee in that pot.'

'I'll pour it,' said Jake.

'Thought you might,' said Milly.

She bustled over to the cooker.

'Get going on your cereal while I do some eggs. He could be ages.'

But DI Henderson was back within a minute.

'More coffee?' Milly said to him.

'No, thank you,' he said.

He sat down at the table and looked across at Maya, his face as grave as before.

'Maya's having breakfast,' said Milly. 'No talking till she's done.'

'Of course,' said the officer.

Maya watched him, sensing his impatience.

'What is it?' she said.

DI Henderson glanced at Milly, then leaned forward on the table.

'Maya,' he said, 'when you've finished your breakfast and Doctor Wade's checked over your bandage, I'd like you to come with me. I've just spoken to your parents and they've said it's all right.'

The officer paused, then turned to Jake.

'And I'd like you to come too, young man.'

27

The hospital at Cresswell had two police cars outside it. WPC Becket was standing by one of them. DI Henderson parked next to her and lowered the window.

'Is he here?' he said.

The policewoman leaned down.

'Yes, sir. Looking nervous.'

'I bet he is.'

Maya glanced at Jake, sitting next to her on the back seat. Neither had spoken during the journey from The Rowan Tree, apart from a few abortive attempts to prise information from DI Henderson. All the officer had said was that Zep was now in custody.

'Are you going to tell us more now?' said Jake.

DI Henderson twisted round in his seat.

'Let's go inside,' he said.

They climbed out of the car and made their way into the hospital. Inside the entrance were DC Coker and a nurse. The policeman saw DI Henderson and stepped forward.

'He's here, sir.'

'So I gather,' said DI Henderson.

He looked round at Maya and Jake.

'I'm not being deliberately mysterious.'

'You could have fooled us,' said Jake.

'I've brought you to the hospital,' said the officer, 'because there are people here I think you'd prefer to see rather than just be told about. There's also been an unexpected development and this seems as appropriate a place as any to follow it up.'

'Meaning what?' said Jake.

But DI Henderson simply turned to the nurse.

'Mo first, I think. Is that OK?'

'Sure,' said the nurse.

And she led them down the corridor.

Maya looked around her and in spite of the clinical brightness of the hospital, she found images of the forest rushing back: the clearing, the beech tree, the thicket, the dusk—and Mo, lying in his own blood.

His strange eyes swirling up at her.

And suddenly here they were again, but now Mo was in a hospital bed and there was no blood, just a huge bandage round his neck; and he was not alone. Bonny was sitting on the bed, wearing a hospital gown, and holding one of the boy's hands. She saw them approaching and jumped off the bed.

'Keep your distance,' she snapped.

The nurse stopped them, well back from the bed.

'Easy, Bonny,' she said. 'Only friends here.'

Bonny squared up to them.

'Mo doesn't like crowds,' she said. 'They spook him.'

She ran her eyes over them.

'Maya can come,' she said. 'But nobody else.'

The nurse drew them off a few feet, turned her back on Bonny, and lowered her voice.

'I'm sorry about this,' she said. 'Bonny's not supposed to be here at all. She's meant to be recovering in another ward. They brought her in looking half-dead, but the moment she knew Mo was here, that was it. We can't keep her away from him. But I'll tell you something strange.'

'Mo's started to get better,' said Maya.

'Yes,' said the nurse. 'He picked up the moment she was there. And he was touch and go, I'm telling you. We all thought we were going to lose him. But now look at him.'

Maya turned back to the bed. Bonny was still standing guard, glaring at them. Behind her was Mo's huge form. Maya stared. The boy's face was turned towards her and though the eyes still swirled, she knew he was watching her.

She started to walk towards him. Bonny's eyes fixed upon her but she ignored them and continued, watching Mo's face all the while. The boy was breathing hard and as she drew near she saw he was holding himself rigid, and fully aware of her.

She stopped by the bed and looked down at him.

'You got one minute,' said Bonny. 'That's all.'

'I don't need a minute,' she said.

She leaned down and kissed Mo on the forehead, then straightened up.

Bonny spoke again.

'I didn't use to like you. But you're all right.'

Maya went on watching Mo.

'You're all right too,' she said quietly.

And she turned and walked away, not looking back.

Bryn and Annie were in separate wards, both sleeping.

'They've come through well,' said the nurse, 'but it was a very close call. Another half hour lying unattended and they might not have made it. Bryn very nearly died in the ambulance. But they're doing OK now.'

DC Coker chuckled.

'They might make it to the wedding yet,' he said.

The nurse looked at him, then at DI Henderson, and Maya saw an unspoken question in the woman's eyes. DI Henderson answered it with a nod; and Maya knew that

200

the time had come for the real purpose of this visit.

She'd already sensed what that was. What she couldn't work out was why it involved Jake. But now they were walking again, the nurse leading them up stairs and through doors, and then down a long, silent corridor towards a closed door at the end.

A policewoman was standing outside it.

In front of her was a figure pacing the floor.

McMurdo.

'Uncle Frank!' called Jake.

The forester looked round but went on walking up and down. Jake hurried on ahead.

'What are you doing here?' he said.

McMurdo didn't answer but he stopped pacing and waited for them to arrive. Maya studied the forester's face. This had to be the man WPC Becket had mentioned earlier. She'd said he looked nervous, but that wasn't true at all. He looked terrified.

She glanced at the closed door, aware of what lay in the room beyond.

'What's going on, Uncle Frank?' said Jake.

McMurdo threw a glance at DI Henderson.

'Tell him, Frank,' said the policeman. 'Exactly what you told DC Coker at the station.'

'I'm sorry, Jake,' said McMurdo. 'I should have told you a long time ago. I just . . . didn't think it could do any good. You knowing.'

'Knowing what?' said Jake.

'That you're not an only child.'

Jake stared at him.

'Is this for real?'

'I've let you down,' said McMurdo. 'I know I have.'

'Go on, Frank,' said DC Coker.

The forester looked down at the floor.

'I hear you caught Zep,' he muttered.

'Yes,' said DI Henderson, 'and he's told us pretty much everything. But Jake needs to hear some of this from you. So does Maya, I reckon.'

'I know, I know.'

McMurdo frowned, then turned to Maya.

'I don't know if Jake's told you,' he said, 'but his dad—Hal—was my brother. Hal and Chloe—Jake's mum—they used to own The Rowan Tree. Before Mr and Mrs Flint came along. Jake doesn't remember either of his parents because he lost them by the time he was two. And he's been living with me ever since.'

Maya said nothing. Her mind was on the room beyond the door.

Even as she listened to the forester.

'No point beating about the bush,' he said. 'The marriage was a disaster. My brother had a drink problem. And he was a difficult bastard, no question. But Chloe was worse. Everybody said that, not just me. Unstable, manipulative, cranky, and a snob. And she had a thing about The Rowan Tree. It was her place, her domain, her bloody kingdom.'

McMurdo looked at Jake.

'This is the bit I should have told you,' he said. 'You won't remember any of it. You were too young. But your parents' marriage was over. They were just screaming at each other all the time. They'd had you but that was the only good thing about the marriage, and they didn't look after you properly. I had to step in lots of times to check you were OK and getting fed and stuff. Half the time you weren't. Hal was drinking hard and Chloe was acting lady of the manor and swanning round The Rowan Tree. And then she took a fancy to a new boy I'd just taken on as my assistant. Called Bryn.'

'Oh, Christ,' said Jake.

'Exactly,' said the forester. 'He was quite a catch back then. Good looking, strong, handy, bit rough, and very innocent. He was nineteen years old. She was in her forties.'

'You could be talking about Zep and Rebecca Flint,' said DC Coker.

'Don't think it hasn't crossed my mind,' said McMurdo. He turned back to Jake.

'It was only a one-night stand, so Bryn told me, but it did the damage. She got pregnant, told Hal, mocked him about it, said it was someone else's baby. He'd have known that anyway. So what does he do? He goes off and sells The Rowan Tree to spite her. Does it in secret. Everything was in his name. He'd started the business before he got married. So he sold the hotel to Mr and Mrs Flint. Then he told Chloe what he'd done and mocked her back.'

Jake looked away.

'I'm sorry, Jake,' said McMurdo. 'I know I should have told you.'

'Does Bryn know?' he said. 'About getting my mum pregnant?'

'I didn't tell him,' said McMurdo. 'Don't think she did either. He's never mentioned it. But I know she had a bad effect on him. Like I say, she wasn't stable and it scared him. He kept away from her after that one night and he's been wary of women ever since. Till he started going out with Annie Shaw.'

'What else haven't you told me?' said Jake.

'Your mum and dad had a massive row. There was some violence. She stormed off and never came back. Hal drank himself into the ground and a few weeks later he fell over outside The Rose and Crown and hit his head on the water trough. Died soon after. In this very hospital.'

'I know most of that,' said Jake. 'What about my mother?'

The forester took a heavy breath.

'I heard nothing from Chloe for thirteen years,' he said. 'That's the truth, Jake. Not a word. Then last year I got a message. A scrawled note. It just gave her name and, well, you couldn't call it an address, more a location. I knew it meant she was in trouble. She was miles away, down on the coast. I didn't say anything to anybody. Maybe I should have, but I didn't. I thought it best not to. I went down to the coast, found your mum living under a bridge. She was all on her own, no money, no food, not even a blanket, and she'd lost it. I'm sorry, Jake. Didn't know who she was or where she was or who I was. She died while I was with her. Just her and me. Under that stinking bridge.'

'Bloody hell,' said Jake.

'And then I did something else wrong,' said McMurdo. 'I meant for the best. It was to protect you. Only you're going to say I should have told you. But I just reported her death to the police like she was some old woman I found lying under a bridge. Like she was no one I knew. So I gave no name, and I don't think they ever got a name for her. I don't even know what happened after. The police took a statement from me and I heard nothing more.'

'So who wrote that note to you?' said Jake. 'It can't have been my mum. If she wasn't right in the head. It must have been someone else.'

McMurdo didn't answer.

'Could her kid have written it?' said Jake.

'Don't ask me,' said McMurdo.

There was a silence. Maya looked at the door, and then stepped over to the nurse.

'Can we go in now?' she said.

'I think we should,' said the nurse.

Jake walked up to Maya and stood beside her. She saw the fear in his face and took his hand. He squeezed hers tight, then looked round at DI Henderson.

'Is the fox-figure in that room?' he said.

'Yes,' said the officer.

'And is the fox-figure my mother's kid?'

'Yes.'

Jake turned towards the door.

'Let's go.'

28

There was only one bed in the room and the figure in it was hidden by the monitors and other equipment cluttered round and by the three nurses standing there. Jake and Maya walked forward together, the others close behind, and as they drew near, the nurses stepped to the side.

And there she was.

A girl of about fifteen.

Eyes closed, body still. Quietly breathing.

Maya stared, wondering.

'I've never seen this girl,' said Jake. 'Has anyone?'

'None of the police officers have,' said DI Henderson.

'I've seen her,' said Maya.

She felt them all look at her, but she went on staring at the girl. The face seemed serene. Yes, that was the word: serene, dangerously serene. Just as it had been in the forest that day, when Zep had risen from the bushes, and this girl had risen a moment later, casually buttoning her shirt and shaking her black hair, before pulling on her jeans and sloping into the trees.

To be forgotten.

Until now.

The black hair lay still upon the sheets. The eyelids remained closed. And Maya was glad. She did not want to see under them.

'Maya?' said Jake. 'Where have you seen this girl?'

'In the forest,' she said. 'I was out with Tom. I had this horrible effigy thing I told you about, the thing I found under the floorboards in my room. I wanted to get rid of it, but I didn't want Tom to see it, so I waited till he wasn't looking, then I threw it towards some bushes. And Zep suddenly stood up. He was in there, in the bushes, and this girl was with him. She was buttoning up her shirt and stuff. But she just walked straight off, all casual, and we didn't take much notice of her because Zep was coming for us. So I kind of . . . forgot about her. Specially as people said Zep's always got lots of girls hanging round him.'

'Her name's Crystal,' said DI Henderson.

Maya looked round at him.

'She's Bryn's daughter and Jake's half-sister,' he said. 'We've learned most of what we need to know about her from Zep. Seems she was so confident of her power over him that she told him everything, or pretty much. All the things she'd done, and all the things she planned to do. And he didn't seem to notice he was being used as a diversion to keep our attention away from her, and the fall guy if it went wrong. Maybe he did notice and just didn't care. He's wild enough. He certainly knew what Crystal was up to. But like I say, she had the power and he didn't.'

Maya looked at the girl's face again.

'Has she spoken at all?' said Jake.

'Not a word,' said one of the nurses. 'She's been in the coma since they found her lying in the forest.'

'Will she live?' said DC Coker.

'Difficult to say,' said the nurse. 'She may come out of it. But Zep hit her very hard.'

'Why did she start killing people?' said Jake.

'Because she's sick,' said McMurdo, 'and psychotic.'

'We can only go on what Zep's told us,' said DI Henderson, 'and he got it all from Crystal, so it's a little speculative. We've found no record of Chloe's movements after she left Hembury all those years ago, and nothing about a daughter called Crystal. Not even a birth certificate. According to Zep, Crystal said she and her mother travelled all the time, living rough, her mother getting more and more ill, and more and more bitter.'

The officer paused.

'I guess that all fed into the girl,' he went on, 'and by the time Chloe died, Crystal was ready to take her revenge.'

'But on who?' said Jake. 'My dad was dead. And Bryn . . . he's her father. And she must have known that. I can't believe my mother wouldn't have told her. So why kill your own dad? And then all the other people?'

'I think it's more complex than that,' said DI Henderson. 'Who's to know what kind of a story Chloe gave the girl? I'm guessing she painted a pretty foul picture of your father, but she wouldn't have spared Bryn either. She probably made him out to be some kind of predator who took advantage of her.'

'Then what about Annie Shaw?' said Jake. 'She hadn't done anything.'

'She was going out with Bryn,' said the officer, 'and ready to get married. What better revenge on Bryn than to kill her too?'

'OK,' said Jake, 'so what about Maya's family? And Mrs Flint? What had they done?'

'Jake,' said Maya.

He looked at her.

'It was The Rowan Tree,' she said. 'Like I told you before. It was an obsession.'

'Whose obsession?'

'Chloe's,' she said. 'Your mother's. She thought The Rowan Tree was hers. Like Mr McMurdo said. She thought it was her kingdom. So Crystal did too.'

She looked at the figure in the bed.

'Maya's right,' said DI Henderson. 'The Rowan Tree's a big factor in all this.'

'Crystal slept in the hotel,' said Maya.

'We know,' said the officer. 'Zep told us. I suspect she wrote the note to Frank, telling him where Chloe was. It was a last act for her dying mum. Then she headed to Hembury. Found The Rowan Tree was empty. Rebecca Flint and her husband had split up and gone, and the place was up for sale. The Munros hadn't moved in yet. So Crystal did instead. In secret.'

McMurdo shook his head.

'How come she did all that and no one saw her?' he said.

'She was clever,' said DI Henderson, 'and very determined. She wanted The Rowan Tree for her mum's sake. And for herself. It's hard to picture this girl walking through that empty place in the dark, sleeping on bare boards. But I guess that's what she did.'

'She slept in my room,' said Maya. 'I could feel . . . something horrible there. It scared me. It still scares me. It's stopped me going back in my room. I know it's where she dreamt of murder. That's what the effigy was for. And the images she cut out of the trees. And the mutilated animals. They were sacrificed as a kind of ritual.'

'For what?' said Jake.

She looked at him.

'For power,' she said. 'For what was to come.'

She thought of the dead foxes; and then the living one. For some reason it felt close again.

She looked into Crystal's face. The eyes were still closed, the features calm. The breathing went on, soft as before.

'I still can't work out how everything fits together,' said Jake.

'I reckon it went something like this,' said DI Henderson. 'Crystal thought: check out The Rowan Tree first, then find a way to kill Bryn. So she got to Hembury, found The Rowan Tree was empty, broke in, and then had a stealthy look round. Worked out pretty quick that Zep was just the mug she needed, hooked him good and proper, and got him to tell her everything she wanted to know. Who's who and what's going on. Found out Bryn was dating Annie Shaw and it was looking serious. So Annie goes on the hit list too. Then Maya's family turn up and now The Rowan Tree's got people in it, new owners. So the Munros go on the hit list. And pretty soon it's anybody who's got any connection with The Rowan Tree. Even previous owners like Rebecca Flint. Crystal wants 'em all dead.'

'Jesus,' said McMurdo.

'But what about Mo?' said Jake. 'Why him?'

'According to Bonny,' said the officer, 'Mo knew who was behind the trouble. Maybe he did. Maybe he saw Crystal in the forest doing something to the trees, or cutting up one of the foxes. Who knows? He's never going to tell us, is he? But it could well be the reason why Crystal tried to kill him.'

There was a long silence. All that broke it was the soft, regular breathing from the figure in the bed. Maya thought of Mum and Dad and Tom, back at The Rowan Tree. She hoped they were sleeping too, and breathing just as quietly.

Jake shook his head.

'Mrs Flint never should have died,' he said.

'She was a mistake,' said DI Henderson.

Jake turned and stared at him.

'You mean . . . Crystal killed her by accident?'

'Oh, no,' said the officer. 'Crystal killed her deliberately.'

'Very deliberately,' said DC Coker.

DI Henderson gave him a disapproving look and continued.

'Rebecca Flint was killed on purpose,' he said. 'When I say her death was a mistake, I mean that Crystal miscalculated its effect.'

'I don't understand,' said Jake.

'It's very simple,' said the officer. 'She had Zep right where she wanted him. He knew she was planning to kill Bryn and Annie, and the Munros. She told him that. Told him about killing Mo too. That's how she found out where Mo and Bonny were hanging out. Zep told her he'd seen Mo at the old barn.'

'But what about Mrs Flint?' said Jake.

'Crystal didn't tell Zep about that. She knew Zep and Mrs Flint were having a fling, but she kept quiet and just went ahead and did it. And that was her mistake. She probably thought she could handle any trouble from Zep. I wouldn't be surprised if she planned to kill him too eventually. Once he'd served his purpose. But like I say, she miscalculated. He found out about Rebecca Flint's death—not from Crystal—but from local talk, or the news, or whatever. And he went after Crystal.'

'But Zep was at the place where Mrs Flint was buried,' said Maya, 'that time he chased me over the fields. He must have known about her.'

'We've spoken to him about that,' said DI Henderson. 'He says he didn't know about the body or even see it. He just saw you and chased you. Says it was a bit of fun.'

'It wasn't,' she said.

'I know that,' said the officer, 'but the point about Rebecca Flint's death is that it drove Zep to anger, made him go after Crystal. Because obviously he knew she was the one who'd done it. I think in a weird kind of way he did actually care for Rebecca Flint.'

Maya turned away, from him, from the others, from the bed. Somehow she couldn't bear to look at Crystal any more. She took a few steps away and stood there, staring at the blank wall of the hospital ward, aware of Tom's face in her mind, and Mum's, and Dad's, and the slow movement of tears down her cheeks.

And she saw the forest again, opening before her.

The clearing, the trees, the thicket.

But no bodies. Not any more.

'Someone's going to die,' she whispered.

She stood there, aware once more of the others behind her, watching her perhaps, or the figure of Crystal in the bed; she didn't know. None were speaking. She listened to the silence behind her; and then suddenly understood.

She turned back to the bed. The others were standing round it, looking down. Only Jake was watching her. She walked back and stood beside him, and they looked down together. The figure was still. As serene as before.

But no longer dangerous.

The breathing had stopped.

29

'Are you sure about this?' said Jake. 'I'd rather come with you.'

She stared past the church at the forest beyond, and shook her head.

'I want to do it by myself,' she said.

'But do you know the way?'

'I can find it.'

She saw the anxiety in his face.

'Tell Mum and Dad I won't be long,' she said, 'and tell them I'm OK. If they give you a hard time for not coming with me, just . . . '

She shrugged.

'Just say something.'

She kissed him on the cheek, hesitated, then kissed him quickly on the mouth and hurried off towards the forest. He called after her.

'Maya.'

She kept walking.

'Maya.'

'I'll be fine, I'll be fine.'

She glanced back, smiled, and pushed on. She wasn't sure of the way, in spite of what she'd told Jake, but to her surprise and relief, she found, once she had left the village behind her and was over the stile and into the trees, that the direction was obvious.

She stopped, wondering why this should be so. Certainly

213

the forest no longer felt hostile, yet it didn't explain why she felt so confident about where to go. She walked on, birdsong breaking out all around her. To the right was one of the defaced trees.

She kept walking, her eyes upon it. A squirrel was running up the trunk. It skittered over the headless image and on to the first branch. She walked on. More trees, more images ripped from the bark. She left them all behind, her mind on Mum and Dad, and Tom.

And Jake.

Here at last was the clearing.

As easy to find as Hembury church.

She stopped and looked over it. All was still. The sun was cutting across the branches of the damaged beech tree. She walked over to the spot where Bryn had lain dying and stood there for a few moments, then wandered over to the thicket where Annie had been, and stopped again.

A wood pigeon called, somewhere near.

She made her way back to the centre of the clearing, then over to the trees at the top. There was the place where she'd stood over Mo. She walked slowly up to it. The grass seemed flattened where the boy had been. She took a slow breath, and turned.

But no figure was there now.

She walked up to the spot where Crystal had stood.

And she closed her eyes.

The wood pigeon called again.

She stayed there, listening to the sounds of the forest, then she opened her eyes again and set off back to The Rowan Tree. She found exactly what she'd expected in the reception area: Tom sitting in a chair, staring towards the door.

He looked pale and weak but he struggled to his feet.

'Sis,' he said.

'I'm all right, Tommy.'

She walked up to him. He stared at her, frowning.

'I could have killed Jake,' he said.

'I think you might have struggled,' she said. 'Jake's stronger than he looks. And you're not well yet.'

'Don't joke about it.'

'It's not Jake's fault,' she said. 'He wanted to come with me. He really did. But I told him he couldn't. I had to do it myself.'

He watched her, still frowning.

'I'm OK, Tommy,' she said.

'If you say so.'

He slumped back in the chair. She heard footsteps down the corridor and saw Milly, Roxy, and Jake hurrying towards her.

'Jake,' she said, 'did you get into trouble?'

'Only with Tom,' he said.

She looked at Tom and shook her head.

'Don't blame Tom for being worried,' said Jake. 'I'd be the same if I were your brother.'

Roxy giggled.

'Aren't you glad you're not?'

'Cut it out,' said Jake.

'Maya,' said Milly. 'You daft girl.'

'I had to go.'

'I know you did,' said Milly, 'but that's you done with wandering off, OK? You can wander into the conservatory now and see your mum and dad.'

'Are they all right?'

'They're flaked out,' said Milly, 'same as Tom is. Doctor Wade just left. She's looking in again tomorrow. Rest needed for everyone, she says. Your head hurting?'

'A bit.'

'Come here. Doctor said I got to check that bandage.'

Milly looked briskly over it.

'Fine,' she said. 'Now go and see your mum and dad.'

They were lying on the sofa, flopped against each other. But they looked up at the same moment and saw her.

'Maya,' said Dad.

She hurried forward. Mum and Dad eased apart and she squeezed onto the sofa between them.

'I'm sorry,' she said. 'I've been—'

'We know where you've been,' said Dad. 'Jake told us.'

'Are you angry with me?'

'Too tired to be angry,' said Dad.

She looked at him.

'We're not angry,' he said.

He kissed her.

'Jake told us about Crystal too.'

Maya leaned back, picturing the girl's face.

And then the clearing again. Silent and still.

'We're going to be all right,' said Mum. 'All of us. We're going to come through.'

'I know,' said Maya.

Roxy appeared in the doorway.

'Milly's making you some tea,' she said.

'Thanks, Roxy,' said Dad. 'Let's all have some. You three come and join us.'

'OK,' said Roxy. 'I'll bring everything in here, shall I?'

'That'll be great,' said Dad.

And Roxy was gone.

'I'll get Tom,' said Maya.

She made her way back down the corridor. From the kitchen came the clink of cups and the sound of Milly humming. Tom was still slumped in the chair by the reception desk. He glanced up at her, his face as drawn as before.

'Are you all right?' she said.

'I was scared,' he said. 'When you went off again.'

'I'm sorry, Tommy.'

'I hate you, sis.'

'No, you don't,' she said.

The phone rang in the office behind the desk.

'Let it ring,' said Tom. 'Milly'll get it.'

Maya hesitated, then stepped into the office and picked it up.

'Hello?' she said.

'Is that The Rowan Tree?'

It was a man's voice. Quiet, cultured.

'Yes,' she said.

'Ah, good,' said the man. 'I was wondering whether you might have a double room for the fifth to the seventh of next month. I realize it's a bit short notice and you're probably booked up already, but—'

'No, we're . . . I mean . . . '

She gripped the phone, aware that Tom had stood up and was watching her from the reception area, and that Roxy and Jake and Milly had joined him.

'Are you there?' said the man.

'Yes,' she said. She glanced quickly through the diary. 'Yes, we . . . we do have a double room for those dates.'

'Oh, that's great,' said the man. 'It's for my wife and myself. We haven't been to your part of the country before but we have some friends who say it's very picturesque.'

'Yes, it's . . . ' She swallowed hard. 'It's very . . . picturesque.'

'Hembury's a village, isn't it?'

'Yes,' she said, 'it's . . . it's quite small but . . . there's an old church and a forest nearby, where you and your wife could go walking. And there's a good pub where you can have meals.'

217

'But you do meals at The Rowan Tree, don't you?' said the man. 'I'm sure I read that on your website.'

'Yes, we do.'

Maya looked at Milly, now standing next to her in the office. Milly smiled at her; and the man spoke again.

'Sounds fine,' he said. 'Can you give me some prices?'

She talked him through the costs, the others still watching.

'OK,' said the man, 'let's go with that. Bed and breakfast and we'll add on other meals as we go. Let me just give you some contact details.'

'OK.'

Maya listened, writing everything down.

'Have you got enough there?' said the man.

'Yes,' said Maya. 'I'll send you an email to confirm the booking. But . . . I didn't get your name.'

'Oh, I beg your pardon,' said the man. 'Nixon. Mr and Mrs Nixon.'

'Nixon,' she said, writing it in the diary.

'And your name is?'

'Maya,' she said. 'Maya Munro.'

'It's a pleasure talking to you, Maya,' said Mr Nixon. 'I look forward to meeting you.'

She put down the phone and found she was trembling. Milly took her by the hand.

'Come on, girl,' she said. 'Let's all have some tea.'

They stayed till late in the evening, Milly, Roxy, and Jake, and Maya was glad of it. Mum and Dad had turned in early, and Tom too, and she felt nervous again with night coming on.

'Are you sure?' said Milly, standing with her on the doorstep. 'I can stay over. No problem at all.'

Maya shook her head.

'I'm fine,' she said. 'I can look after them.'

218

'They're sleeping well,' said Milly, 'and Doctor Wade did say that's what they need more than anything. But listen. You got my number, OK? Any problems, you give me a ring. And I'll be here in five minutes.'

'Thanks.'

Milly glanced at Roxy and Jake.

'Come on, you two.'

And they set off down the lane. Maya stood in the open door, watching Milly and Roxy walk on ahead, and Jake dawdle, glancing back. She stepped out into the lane and he stopped at once. She walked up to him and saw him smile.

Milly's voice floated back on the still air.

'Come on, Jakey.'

Jake rolled his eyes.

'You better go,' said Maya.

'I'll see you,' he said.

And he ran off down the lane after the others.

She waited till they'd disappeared from view, then stepped inside The Rowan Tree, locked the front door, and walked round, checking all the other doors, and the windows, and turning lights off as she went.

Mum and Dad were back in their own room, and Tom was in his, all three fast asleep. She watched them for a while, then fetched her night clothes from Room Nine and carried them down the corridor to her bedroom.

The door faced her as before. She looked at it, then reached out and pushed it open. The room seemed to stare out at her. She stepped in, closed the door, and stood there for a few moments, then changed into her night clothes and climbed into bed.

All was silent.

She switched off the light, lay back, and waited. Midnight, one o'clock, half past. Then she heard it. The growl. Low in the night. She listened, wondering why she wasn't scared any more. The growl came again.

She climbed out of bed, walked to the window overlooking the lane, and drew back the curtains. All was dark outside. No lights in the village at all. She opened the window and stared out; and there they were, just below her.

The two yellow eyes, peering up.

She leaned on the sill and watched them.

And as she did so, they closed, opened, closed again.

And were gone.

Tim Bowler is one of the UK's most compelling and original writers for teenagers. He was born in Leigh-on-Sea and after studying Swedish at university, he worked in forestry, the timber trade, teaching and translating before becoming a full-time writer. He lives with his wife in a small village in Devon and his workroom is an old stone outhouse known to friends as 'Tim's Bolthole'.

Tim has written eighteen books and won fifteen awards, including the prestigious Carnegie Medal for *River Boy,* and his provocative *BLADE* series is being hailed as a groundbreaking work of fiction. He has been described by the *Sunday Telegraph* as 'the master of the psychological thriller' and by the *Independent* as 'one of the truly individual voices in British teenage fiction'.

Questions from readers:

Q. Where do you get your ideas from?

A. Sometimes you have to go looking for ideas. Other times they creep up behind you and tap you on the shoulder and force you to write about them. Somebody once said that writers don't have ideas—ideas have writers. In other words, the idea becomes so powerful it starts to possess the writer. There's something in that. The main thing is to be alive to what's going on around you and—more importantly— what's going on inside you. Sometimes a picture in your head sets you off, or a character from real life, or a person you make up, or a melody, or a smell, or an invented situation. It can be anything that sets your mind racing.

Q. What inspired you to be an author?

A. Reading and writing. Reading authors like Enid Blyton, Arthur Ransome, Rosemary Sutcliff and others, and then trying to write my own stories. It was such good fun I decided I wanted to carry on doing it. And I still am.

Q. Many of your books are set in isolated places. Why is this?

A. I love isolated places. I love wild places, places with a powerful atmosphere. A location is like another character in the story. It has its own personality and that personality impacts on the story just as the characters do. Isolated locations are particularly evocative because they place the characters in isolation, too, where they are often at their most vulnerable. Some people thrive in lonely spots; others fall to pieces. Isolation can bring out fear and it can also bring out courage. The surroundings are a vital element to the story and if well drawn can both reflect and deepen the conflict that the characters are acting out before us.

Q. Which of your books is your favourite?

A. I haven't got a favourite. It's like asking a parent which is his/her favourite child. I feel differently about each book but there isn't one I like best.

Q. Do you have a special place where you like to write?

A. I can write practically anywhere and I do lots of writing in hotel rooms when I'm travelling but when I'm at home, I have two places where I like to work. One is a converted upstairs bedroom that overlooks the churchyard and has a beautiful view of the green hills beyond. My wife calls the room Tim's Dream Factory. Mostly, however, I work in an old outhouse at the top of the village. It's a little place that I use just for writing and thinking. There's nothing in there except a desk, a chair, a light and a power socket for my computer and the electric fire. It's a primitive little den and I love it. My family and friends call it Tim's Bolthole.

Q. There is a dark side to many of your books which is part of their attraction. Did you put this in deliberately or did it just happen?

A. It just happened but so many people have asked me why that I've been forced to ponder the matter. I write from instinct and follow what feels right to me but I think probably the answer to the question is that the stories I write are my way of facing evil. I write about the dark side not to glorify but to confront it.

Q. I want to write and publish a book but every time I write a story I get bored and stop writing it altogether. Can you help me?

A. There's no easy answer to your question except to say: stick with it. I think you need to get a complete draft of the story in front of you. Sometimes, it's true, you have to ditch a story halfway through if you really find it's not going the way you want it to, but in your case you say you stop because you're bored, not necessarily because you think the story is going in the wrong direction. Unfortunately you have to be a bit stubborn and persistent to make it as a writer. Getting bored is a problem but the solution lies with you. If you genuinely want to write (you may need to ask yourself if you do), then you have to make yourself push on and finish the story, come what may. Good luck.

Find out more about Tim, his writing, and read more questions and answers at www.timbowler.co.uk.

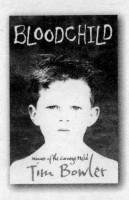

Will lies in a deserted lane. All he knows is that he's had an accident and that his life is slipping away. Against all odds he survives—but with an almost total loss of memory. He does not even know himself.

And that is not all. Why does he have so many enemies? And who is the strange child who seems to have a story to tell him?
Something terrifying has happened in this town. Will can sense it, but he can't remember . . . and searching for the answers is a dangerous task.

For the town has a secret and there are those who will do anything to preserve it.

Even kill.

'Reminded me of Stephen King at his best. It's convincing, atmospheric and creepy.'
Charlie Higson, *The Mail on Sunday*

When Dusty gets the phone call from a mysterious boy she knows she can't ignore it. He seems to know something about the disappearance of her brother, Josh, which means that Dusty must find the boy no matter what.

But when she does finally meet him, there's something strange and haunting about him. He can see people's thoughts, and feels everything—from chilling ice to white-hot pain . . . and he seems to have a hold over everyone he meets.

There's talk in the town of the boy's past. Lynch mobs are out to get him. Dusty must help him and find out what happened to Josh.
But when the mob turns on her, it is she, and not the boy, who is in the gravest danger . . .

'Tim Bowler is master of the psychological thriller and teens won't find a more atmospherically gripping opener than that of *Frozen Fire* . . . and the tension never lets up.'
Sunday Telegraph